THE INVENTION
OF MOREL

ADOLFO BIOY CASARES

Translated by
RUTH L. C. SIMMS

Prologue by
JORGE LUIS BORGES

Introduction by
SUZANNE JILL LEVINE

Illustrated by
NORAH BORGES DE TORRE

NEW YORK REVIEW BOOKS

New York

This is a New York Review Book
Published by The New York Review of Books
207 East 32nd Street, New York, NY 10016
www.nyrb.com

Library of Congress Cataloging-in-Publication Data
Bioy Casares, Adolfo
  [Invención de Morel. English]
  The invention of Morel / by Adolfo Bioy Casares ; translated by Ruth
  L.C. Simms ; prologue by Jorge Luis Borges ; introduction by Suzanne
  Jill Levine.
      p. cm. — (New York Review Books classics)
  ISBN 1-59017-057-1 (pbk. : alk. paper)
  I. Simms, Ruth L.C. II. Title. III. Series.
  PQ7797.B535I6 2003
  863'.62—dc22

                                        2003015601

ISBN 978-1-59017-057-1

Book design by Lizzie Scott
Printed in the United States of America on acid-free paper.
20 19 18 17 16

CONTENTS

INTRODUCTION

THE ARGENTINE Adolfo Bioy Casares (1914–1999) inspired generations of Latin American readers and writers with his stories and novels rich with "reasoned imagination," prophetic fantasies, elegant humor, and stoic ironies about romantic love. Bioy, as he was called by friends and peers, began writing within the cosmopolitan sphere of *Sur* magazine—founded by the influential Victoria Ocampo—in Buenos Aires in the early 1930s. In this stimulating environment, surrounded not only by Argentine but by international cultural figures from Europe (including Spanish poets and intellectuals who were fleeing the Civil War), North America, and Asia, it was the friendship of Jorge Luis Borges that led the young Bioy to develop into the consummate literary stylist he became. Indeed Borges prefaced the first edition, in 1940, of *The Invention of Morel*—Bioy Casares's most famous book and undoubtedly a twentieth-century classic—with an impassioned defense of fantastic literature. For Borges and Bioy, the fantastic was a far richer medium compared to what they then considered the impoverished artifices of nineteenth-century realism. Citing *Morel* as a "perfect" contemporary model of the genre, Borges placed the twenty-six-year-old writer's first successful fiction in the company of Henry James's *The Turn of the Screw* and Franz Kafka's *The Trial*.

What was the fantastic in Borgesian terms? The fantastic or "magic" emanates from pre-modern modes of thought; hence fantastic narrative involved the irruption of a "lucid" magical system of causation upon what we know to be "natural" causation, making the reader question the normal boundaries between fantasy and reality. Borges concludes in his 1940 preface: "In Spanish, works of reasoned imagination are infrequent and even very rare.... *The Invention of Morel*...brings a new genre to our land and our language." Octavio Paz, years later, preferred not to pigeonhole Bioy Casares as a fantasist, however. The Nobel Prize–winning Mexican poet and essayist described this intriguing novella and many of Bioy's fictions' principal themes as not cosmic but rather metaphysical:

> The body is imaginary, and we bow to the tyranny of a phantom. Love is a privileged perception, the most total and lucid not only of the unreality of the world but of our own unreality: not only do we traverse a realm of shadows; we ourselves are shadows.

From *The Invention of Morel* to later stories and novels such as *The Adventure of a Photographer in La Plata* (1985), the perception of desire in Bioy's fictions serves to make both protagonist and reader painfully aware of solitude, of the pathetic, tragic, and yet comic ways in which lovers lose one another, of the impossibility of being the heroic master of one's destiny.

Adolfo Bioy Casares was born in Buenos Aires on September 15, 1914, the only child of wealthy parents. Adolfo Bioy, descendant of a French family from Béarn, the southwestern region of France often in the background of his son's stories, was the author of two volumes of memoirs; Marta Casares, considered a great beauty in her day, came from a well-established family, owners of La Martona, the largest dairy chain in the country. It was through Marta Casares's friendship with the Ocampos that her seventeen-year-old son would meet in 1931 his literary mentor Borges, then thirty, and also his wife-to-be, Victoria's sister, the writer and painter Silvina Ocampo. Rincon Viejo, the family ranch in Pardo in the province of Buenos Aires, was to give Bioy and Borges their first pretext to write in collaboration, a pamphlet on the virtues of yogurt!

The familiar image of Bioy Casares as disciple and collaborator of Borges placed him, in the Latin American canon, under the shadow of the maestro. Even though Borges once called Bioy the "secret master" who led him out of his experimentation with baroque metaphors into classical prose, Borges's message was, as always, double: "master" in the sense that children teach their parents. But more than mentor and disciple Borges and Bioy were lifelong friends whose ingenious and passionate discussions of literature and their favorite writers (like Stevenson, Poe, Chesterton, and, of course, Kafka) were mutually nourishing. In poetry, Borges favored the epic, such as Whitman, whereas Bioy favored the lyrical, as in Verlaine.

Love was always to be an endangered and endangering obsession in Bioy: the sweet revelations in the laurel bower can bring down catastrophe, whether that evil be banal stupidity or some divine (or diabolical) wrath. Stories his mother told him as a child provided the blueprint for many of his own fictions:

> My mother tells me stories about animals who stray from the nest, are exposed to danger, and in the end, after many adventures, return to the security of the nest. The theme of the safe, or apparently safe, haven and of the dangers that lurk outside still appeals to me.

Bioy's life was a gentler version of these fables. A shy yet witty, melancholy, and handsome man, he traveled often, mainly to France—a second home and, as for many Latin American intellectuals, a cultural mecca. Despite or because of his timidity, he was a "hero of women" (the apropos title of a later volume of stories).

Bioy's writing obsessively reenacted his early fascination with the ominous adventure. Time and again his hesitant protagonists are thrust headlong—out of some unspelled yet inevitable necessity—into situations they cannot comprehend and whose consequences may be disastrous. H. G. Wells's scientific romance *The Island of Dr. Moreau*, in which a mad scientist turns beasts into men, becomes a kind of leitmotif throughout Bioy's novels, from *Morel* (the name an obvious allusion) and *A Plan for Escape* (1945) to *Asleep in the Sun* (1973). In the latter, the animal metaphor for the human condition becomes literal when good-natured Lucio Bordenave suspects that a sinister doctor has transformed his wife (literally) into a bitch. Lucio's life is completely dissolved when his soul too is transferred into a dog's body.

Friends "explained" the supernatural to Bioy, according to him, at an early age. Bioy described these revelations thus:

> Through cracks that might open at any moment in the earth's crust, a devil might grab you by the foot and drag you down to hell. The supernatural as something terrifying and sad. While we play at throwing a ball against the wall in back of the house, my friend Drago Mitre explains that heaven and hell are the lies of religion. I feel relieved. I would like to go inside a three-way mirror, where the images would repeat themselves clearly. The supernatural as something attractive.

So, for example, what is obviously hell in Edgar Allan Poe's classic story "The Pit and the Pendulum," in which a prisoner of the Inquisition is exposed to the torture of burning, shining walls closing in on him, became in *The Invention of Morel* an allusion to an ambiguous heaven. The mirror which reflects (but also threatens to supplant us) can be sinister or good, fearful or beautiful, depending upon how it is perceived. In Bioy's paradoxical universe the symbol turns upon itself: his texts are filled with tantalizing allusions and symbols which are no longer keys but rather enigmatic ciphers. As the narrator quotes Mallarmé in *A Plan for Escape*, the novella Bioy wrote immediately after *Morel*, "anything is a symbol of anything." His reader experiences an effect of referentiality but there is no reality outside the terrifying or beautiful mirror, outside the text—or the perception.

Bioy wrote and published six books between 1929 and 1940, but he considered (and his critics followed suit) that his real literary production began with *The Invention of Morel*. To entertain friends in later years he would often trot out one of the earlier attempts. He would claim it was written by some young writer, read a section that would be sure to produce mocking laughter, and then reveal that he was the author; of these earlier publications he said: "I publish, my friends look sad and don't know what to say to me." But finally, he had a breakthrough, as he described in a chronology of his life and works:

> At Pardo I glimpse what will be the plot of *The Invention of Morel*. I understand that something is wrong with my way of writing and I tell myself it's time to do something about it. For reasons of caution, in writing the new novel, I don't strive to make a big hit, just to avoid errors.

Bioy's early writings "suffered" from the chaotic influence of Surrealism's "automatic writing" and Joyce's stream-of-consciousness. In Bioy's first conversation with el maestro Borges, the mature writer responded to the young man's enthusiasm for Joyce, emblem of the "modern" and of "total freedom," by suggesting—against the grain—that *Ulysses* was more a promise than an achieved masterpiece. Borges may have brought Bioy to the classical at this early stage, citing Horace and promoting the virtues of narrative rigor, such as to be found in the "superior" plots of G. K. Chesterton. Bioy embraced Borges's poetics of condensation and concision, which favored the speculative and the artificial over the novelist's expansive representation of human experience. By the mere fact of writing novels, however, Bioy would always appear (at least) to be more concerned than Borges with re-creating the "lived and the seen."

Although Bioy had still not discovered his mode in the volume of stories that preceded *Morel*, titled *Luis Greve, Dead* (1937), Borges found in this book the seed of the writer-to-be, as he wrote in his review in *Sur*:

> Our literature is poor in fantastic narratives, preferring the formless *tranche de vie* or the episodic. Which makes Bioy Casares's work unusual. In *Chaos* (1934) and *The New Storm* (1935) imagination predominates; in this book—in the best pages of this book—that imagination obeys an order. "Nothing is so rare as order in the operations of the spirit," said Fenelon. In *Luis Greve* he has begun to master games with time and space which attempt to impose another order—a literary one—upon an absurd universe.

One of the stories in this early volume, "The Postcard Lovers," about a young man who interpolates his image into the photograph of a girl he loves, anticipates *The Invention of Morel*, in which *l'amour fou* is carried to its ultimate consequences. When the girl in the postcard discovers the photograph and the love, her life changes.... *The Invention of Morel* transports this scheme into the realm of science fiction, and away from Argentina to an unknown and supposedly deserted island: Bioy needed to "decontaminate" himself from the subjectivity of his immediate Argentine reality to gain aesthetic distance. But I won't ruin the fun for the reader by revealing the plot, which, as Borges observed, is a magnificent invention, inspired by science fiction ranging from H. G. Wells to Villiers de l'Isle-Adam's *The Future Eve*. I will remark, however, that Bioy's "invention," like all good science fiction, was prophetic, and intuitively predicted future scientific realities.

This meticulously wrought novella of just over one hundred pages was received with acclaim, and brought Bioy recognition beyond the borders of the *Sur* group; he was awarded the first municipal Buenos Aires prize for literature. When translated into French in 1953, its narrative device of two lovers coexisting spatially in two different temporal dimensions would inspire Alain Robbe-Grillet's script for Resnais's film *Last Year at Marienbad* (1961). He would continue to receive literary prizes at home and abroad, and films in Argentina and Europe have been based on his many seductive plots: *The Invention of Morel* has actually been filmed several times, but none of these films seem to capture the elusive charm of this novella about characters who are filmed. Aside from several movie and TV versions made in France, Italy, and Argentina, *Morel* has become a cult reference, as for example in the Argentine Eliseo Subiela's metaphysical film *Man Facing Southeast* (1985). At the same time, among Argentine proponents of realism, *Morel* gained for Bioy the reputation of "clockmaker," of an intellectual enamored of his own mental constructions or "bachelor machines." Lucio Bordenave, the bungling clockmaker in the later *Asleep in the Sun*, was perhaps a burlesque response to this misreading—but even Bioy himself felt that it wasn't until the story "The Idol" in *The Celestial Plot* (1948) that he had "loosened up" and found his style.

Bioy's style is terse and understated: the translation of *The Invention of Morel* by Ruth L. C. Simms, first published in 1964 by the University of Texas Press, tends at times—a common tendency in many translations, even the best—to paraphrase, to create smoother transitions where the original might seem excessively spare. But in general the translation is accurate and faithful to his elegance. Bioy's sentences reflect his tendency in general toward shorter, concise narrative forms; his narrators say less rather than more, inviting one to read between the lines. Their elliptical, matter-of-fact manner of communicating bewilderment makes the reader both laugh at and sympathize with bungling antiheros who don't quite have a grip on reality but are doing their best. Beneath this mild surface, Bioy's elegant textual machines, like the "invention" of the mad scientist Morel, are works of passion, expressing a desire for eternal love and a poignant failure to counter the dissolution wrought by mortality. The young Bioy, in this unforgettable work, had already mastered a lucid irony that maintains distance between the passion with which he would always denounce and the curiosity with which he would invariably register the evils of the world, and especially the fatal limitations of humankind.

—SUZANNE JILL LEVINE
Santa Barbara, California
April 20, 2003

THE INVENTION OF MOREL

To Jorge Luis Borges

PROLOGUE

AROUND 1880 Stevenson noted that the adventure story was regarded as an object of scorn by the British reading public, who believed that the ability to write a novel without a plot, or with an infinitesimal, atrophied plot, was a mark of skill. In *The Dehumanization of Art* (1925) José Ortega y Gasset, seeking the reason for that scorn, said, "I doubt very much whether an adventure that will interest our superior sensibility can be invented today," and added that such an invention was "practically impossible." On other pages, on almost all the other pages, he upheld the cause of the "psychological" novel and asserted that the pleasure to be derived from adventure stories was nonexistent or puerile. This was undoubtedly the prevailing opinion in 1880, 1925, and even 1940. Some writers (among whom I am happy to include Adolfo Bioy Casares) believe they have a right to disagree. The following, briefly, are their reasons.

The first of these (I shall neither emphasize nor attenuate the fact that it is a paradox) has to do with the intrinsic form of the adventure story. The typical psychological novel is formless. The Russians and their disciples have demonstrated, tediously, that no one is impossible. A person may kill himself because he is so happy, for example, or commit murder as an act of benevolence. Lovers may separate forever as a consequence of their love. And one man can inform on another out of fervor or humility. In the end such complete freedom is tantamount to chaos. But the psychological novel would also be a "realistic" novel, and have us forget that it is a verbal artifice, for it uses each vain precision (or each languid obscurity) as a new proof of realism. There are pages, there are chapters in Marcel Proust that are unacceptable as inventions, and we unwittingly resign ourselves to them as we resign ourselves to the insipidity and the emptiness of each day. The adventure story, on the other hand, does not propose to transcribe reality: it is an artificial object, no part of which lacks justification. It must have a rigid plot if it is not to succumb to the mere sequential variety of *The Golden Ass*, the *Seven Voyages of Sinbad*, or the *Quixote*.

I have given one reason of an intellectual sort; there are others of an empirical nature. We hear sad murmurs that our century lacks the ability to devise interesting plots. But no one attempts to prove that if this century has any ascendancy over the preceding ones it lies in the quality of its plots. Stevenson is more passionate, more diverse, more lucid, perhaps more deserving of our unqualified friendship than is Chesterton; but his plots are inferior. De Quincey plunged deep into labyrinths on his nights of meticulously detailed horror, but he did not coin his impression of "unutterable and self-repeating infinities" in fables comparable to Kafka's. Ortega y Gasset was right when he said that Balzac's "psychology" did not satisfy us; the same thing could be said of his plots. Shakespeare and Cervantes were both delighted by the antinomian idea of a girl who, without losing her beauty, could be taken for a man; but we find that idea unconvincing now. I believe I am free from every superstition of modernity, of any illusion that yesterday differs intimately from today or will differ from tomorrow; but I maintain that during no other era have there been novels with such admirable plots as *The Turn of the Screw*, *The Trial*, *Voyage to the Center of the Earth*, and the one you are about to read, which was written in Buenos Aires by Adolfo Bioy Casares.

Detective stories—another popular genre in this century

that cannot invent plots—tell of mysterious events that are later explained and justified by reasonable facts. In this book Adolfo Bioy Casares easily solves a problem that is perhaps more difficult. The odyssey of marvels he unfolds seems to have no possible explanation other than hallucination or symbolism, and he uses a single fantastic but not supernatural postulate to decipher it. My fear of making premature or partial revelations restrains me from examining the plot and the wealth of delicate wisdom in its execution. Let me say only that Bioy renews in literature a concept that was refuted by St. Augustine and Origen, studied by Louis-Auguste Blanqui, and expressed in memorable cadences by Dante Gabriel Rossetti:

> I have been here before,
> But when or how I cannot tell:
> I know the grass beyond the door,
> The sweet keen smell,
> The sighing sound, the lights around the shore.

In Spanish, works of reasoned imagination are infrequent and even very rare. The classics employed allegory, the exaggerations of satire, and, sometimes, simple verbal incoherence. The only recent works of this type I remember are a story in Leopoldo Lugones's *Las fuerzas extrañas* and one by Santiago Dabove: now unjustly forgotten. *The Invention of Morel* (the title alludes filially to another island inventor, Moreau) brings a new genre to our land and our language.

I have discussed with the author the details of his plot. I have reread it. To classify it as perfect is neither an imprecision nor a hyperbole.

—JORGE LUIS BORGES

THE INVENTION OF MOREL

TODAY, on this island, a miracle happened: summer came ahead of time. I moved my bed out by the swimming pool, but then, because it was impossible to sleep, I stayed in the water for a long time. The heat was so intense that after I had been out of the pool for only two or three minutes I was already bathed in perspiration again. As day was breaking, I awoke to the sound of a phonograph record. Afraid to go back to the museum to get my things, I ran away down through the ravine. Now I am in the lowlands at the southern part of the island, where the aquatic plants grow, where mosquitoes torment me, where I find myself waist-deep in dirty streams of sea water. And, what is worse, I realize that there was no need to run away at all. Those people did not come here on my account; I believe they did not even see me. But here I am, without provisions, trapped in the smallest, least habitable part of the island—the marshes that the sea floods once each week.

I am writing this to leave a record of the adverse miracle. If I am not drowned or killed trying to escape in the next few days, I hope to write two books. I shall entitle them *Apology for Survivors* and *Tribute to Malthus*. My books will expose the men who violate the sanctity of forests and deserts; I intend to show that the world is an implacable hell for fugitives, that its efficient police forces, its documents, newspapers, radio broadcasts, and border patrols have made every error of justice irreparable. So far I have written only this one page; yesterday I had no inkling of what was going to happen. There are so many things to do on this lonely island! The trees that grow here have such hard wood! And when I see a bird in flight I realize the vastness of the open spaces all around me!

An Italian rugseller in Calcutta told me about this place. He said (in his own language): "There is only one possible place for a fugitive like you—it is an uninhabited island, but a human being cannot live there. Around 1924 a group of white men built a museum, a chapel, and a swimming pool on the island. The work was completed, and then abandoned."

I interrupted him; I wanted to know how to reach it; the rug merchant went on talking: "Chinese pirates do not go there, and the white ship of the Rockefeller Institute never calls at the island, because it is known to be the focal point of a mysterious disease, a fatal disease that attacks the outside of the body and then works inward. The nails drop off the fingers and toes; the hair falls out. The skin and the corneas of the eyes die, and the body lives on for one week, or two at the most. The crew of a ship that had stopped there were skinless, hairless, without nails on their fingers or toes— all dead, of course—when they were found by the Japanese cruiser *Namura*. The horrified Japanese sank their ship."

But my life was so unbearable that I decided to go there anyway. The Italian tried to dissuade me; but in the end I managed to obtain his help.

Last night, for the hundredth time, I slept in this deserted place. As I looked at the buildings, I thought of what a laborious task it must have been to bring so many stones here. It would have been easy enough—and far more practical—to build an outdoor oven. When I was finally able to sleep, it was very late. The music and the shouting woke me up a few hours later. I have not slept soundly since my escape; I am sure that if a ship, a plane, or any other form of transportation had arrived, I would have heard it. And yet suddenly, unaccountably, on this oppressive summerlike night, the grassy hillside has become crowded with people who dance, stroll up and down, and swim in the pool, as if this were a summer resort like Los Teques or Marienbad.

————

From the marshlands with their churning waters I can see the top of the hill, and the people who have taken up residence in the museum. I suppose someone might attribute their mysterious appearance to the effect of last night's heat on my brain. But there are no hallucinations or imaginings here: I know these people are real—at least as real as I am.

The fact that their clothes are from another era indicates that they are a group of eccentrics; but I have known many people who use such devices to capture the magic of the past.

I watch them unwaveringly, constantly, with the eyes of a man who has been condemned to death. They are dancing on the grassy hillside as I write, unmindful of the snakes at their feet. They are my unconscious enemies who, as they corner me against the sea in the disease-infested marshes, deprive me of everything I need, everything I must have if I am to go on living. The sound of their very loud phonograph—"Tea for Two" and "Valencia" are their favorite records—seems now to be permanently superimposed on the wind and the sea.

Perhaps watching them is a dangerous pastime: like every group of civilized men they no doubt have a network of consular establishments and a file of fingerprints that can send me, after the necessary ceremonies or conferences have been held, to jail.

But I am exaggerating. I actually find a certain fascination in watching these odious intruders—it has been so long since I have seen anyone. But there are times when I must stop.

First of all, I have so much work to do. This place could

kill even a seasoned islander. And I have not been here long; I have no tools to work with.

Secondly, there is always the danger that they may see me watching them, or that they may find me if they come down to this part of the island; so I must build some sort of shelter to hide in.

And, finally, it is very difficult for me to see them. They are at the top of the hill, while I am far below. From here they look like a race of giants—I can see them better when they approach the ravine.

Living on these sandbanks is dreadful at a time like this. A few days ago the tide was higher than any I have seen since I came to the island.

When it grows dark I make a bed of branches covered with leaves. I am never surprised to wake up and find that I am in the water. The tide comes in around seven o'clock in the morning, sometimes earlier. But once a week there are tides that can put an end to everything. I count the days by making gashes in a tree trunk; a mistake would fill my lungs with water.

I have the uncomfortable sensation that this paper is changing into a will. If I must resign myself to that, I shall try to make statements that can be verified so that no one, knowing that I was accused of duplicity, will doubt that they condemned me unjustly. I shall adopt the motto of Leonardo—*Ostinato rigore*—as my own, and endeavor to live up to it.

I believe that this island is called Villings, and belongs to the archipelago of the Ellice Islands.[1] More details can be obtained from the rug merchant, Dalmacio Ombrellieri (21 Hyderabad Street, Ramkrishnapur, Calcutta). He fed me for

---

1. Doubtful. He mentions a hill and several kinds of trees. The Ellice, or Lagoon, Islands are flat. The coconut is the only tree that grows in their coral sands. (Editor's Note.)

several days while I hid in one of his Persian rugs, and then he put me in the hold of a ship bound for Rabaul. (But I do not wish to compromise him in any way, for I am naturally very grateful to him.) My book *Apology for Survivors* will enshrine Ombrellieri in the memory of men—the probable location of heaven—as a kind person who helped a poor devil escape from an unjust sentence.

In Rabaul, a card from the rug merchant put me in contact with a member of Sicily's best-known society. By the moon's metallic gleam (I could smell the stench of the fish canneries), he gave me instructions and a stolen boat. I rowed frantically, and arrived, incredibly, at my destination (for I did not understand the compass; I had lost my bearings; I had no hat and I was ill, haunted by hallucinations). The boat ran aground on the sands at the eastern side of the island (the coral reefs must have been submerged). I stayed in the boat for more than a day, reliving that horrible experience, forgetting that I had arrived at my journey's end.

The island vegetation is abundant. Spring, summer, autumn, and winter plants, grasses, and flowers overtake each other with urgency, with more urgency to be born than to die, each one invading the time and the place of the others in a tangled mass. But the trees seem to be diseased; although their trunks have vigorous new shoots, their upper branches are dry. I find two explanations for this: either the grass is sapping the strength from the soil or else the roots of the trees have reached stone (the fact that the young trees are in good condition seems to confirm the second theory). The trees on the hill have grown so hard that it is impossible to cut them; nor can anything be done with those on the bank: the slightest pressure destroys them, and all that is left is a sticky sawdust, some spongy splinters.

The island has four grassy ravines; there are large boulders in the ravine on the western side. The museum, the chapel, and the swimming pool are up on the hill. The buildings are modern, angular, unadorned, built of unpolished stone, which is somewhat incongruous with the architectural style.

The chapel is flat, rectangular—it looks like a long box. The swimming pool appears to be well built, but as it is at ground level it is always filled with snakes, frogs, and aquatic insects. The museum is a large building, three stories high, without a visible roof; it has a covered porch in front and another smaller one in the rear, and a cylindrical tower.

The museum was open when I arrived; I moved in at once. I do not know why the Italian referred to it as a museum. It could be a fine hotel for about fifty people, or a sanatorium.

In one room there is a large but incomplete collection of books, consisting of novels, poetry, drama. The only exception was a small volume (Bélidor, *Travaux: Le Moulin Perse*, Paris, 1737), which I found on a green-marble shelf and promptly tucked away into a pocket of these now threadbare trousers. I wanted to read it because I was intrigued by the name *Bélidor*, and I wondered whether the *Moulin Perse* would help me understand the mill I saw in the lowlands of this island. I examined the shelves in vain, hoping to find some books that would be useful for a research project I began before the trial. (I believe we lose immortality because we have not conquered our opposition to death; we keep insisting on the primary, rudimentary idea: that the whole body should be kept alive. We should seek to preserve only the part that has to do with consciousness.)

The large room, a kind of assembly hall, has walls of rose-colored marble, with greenish streaks that resemble sunken columns. The windows, with their panes of blue glass, would reach the top floor of the house where I was born. Four alabaster urns (six men could hide in each one) irradiate electric light. The books improve the room somewhat. One door

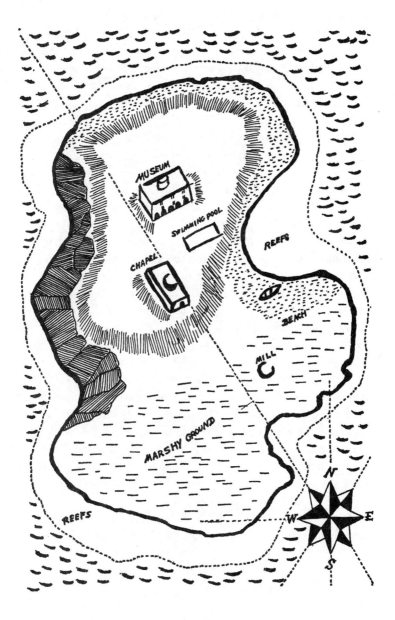

opens onto the hall; another opens onto the round room; another, the smallest one, is concealed by a screen and opens onto a spiral staircase. The principal staircase is at the end of the hall; it is elegantly carpeted. There are some wicker chairs in the room, and the walls are lined with books.

The dining room measures approximately forty feet by fifty. There are three mahogany columns at each side, and each group of columns supports a stand with a figure of a seated divinity that appears to be Indian or Egyptian, of ocher terracotta. Each god is three times larger than a man, and is garlanded by dark plaster leaves. Below them there are large panels with drawings by Foujita, which present a discordant aspect (because of their humility).

The floor of the circular room is an aquarium. Invisible glass boxes in the water incase the electric lights that provide the only illumination for that windowless room. I recall the place with disgust. Hundreds of dead fish were floating on the water when I arrived, and removing them was an obnoxious task. Now, after letting the water run for days and days, I can still smell the odor of dead fish when I am in the room (it reminds me of the beaches in my country, where huge quantities of fish, dead and alive, emerge from the water to contaminate the air, and receive a hasty burial at the hands of the outraged populace). The lighted floor and the black-lacquer columns around it give one the impression of walking magically on top of a pool in the midst of a forest. This room adjoins the large room, or assembly hall, and a small green room with a piano, a phonograph, and a screen of mirrors, which has twenty panels or more.

The rooms are modern, pretentious, unpleasant. There are fifteen suites. Clearing mine out completely made only a slight improvement. There were no more paintings by Picasso, or smoked crystal, or books inscribed by famous people, but still I felt wretched and uncomfortable.

On two occasions I made discoveries in the basement. The first time I was looking for food—the provisions in the storeroom were growing scarce—and I found the power plant. Walking through the basement, I noticed that the skylight I had seen outside, with thick panes of glass and iron grating, partly hidden by the branches of a cedar tree, was not visible from the inside. As if I were involved in an argument with someone who insisted that the skylight was not real, that I had dreamed it, I went outside to see whether it was really there.

It was. I returned to the basement and after some difficulty I got my bearings and found, from the inside, the place that corresponded to the skylight's position. I looked for cracks, secret doors. The search was to no avail, for the wall was smooth and very solid. I thought that the wall must surely conceal a hidden treasure; but when I decided to break the wall to see what was behind it I was motivated by the hope of finding, not machine guns and munitions, but the food I needed so desperately.

I removed an iron bolt from the door, and with increasing weariness, I used it to make a small opening in the wall: a blue light appeared. I worked with a kind of frenzy and soon I made a hole large enough to crawl through. My first reaction was not disappointment at finding no food, or relief at recognizing a water pump and a generator, but ecstatic, prolonged amazement: the walls, the ceiling, the floor were of blue tile and even the air itself (in that room where the only contact with the outside world was a high skylight obscured by the branches of a tree) had the deep azure transparency of a waterfall's foam.

I know very little about motors, but even so I was not long in getting them started. Now when the rain water is all gone I can turn on the pump. It surprises me that the machines are

relatively uncomplicated and in good condition and, especially, that I knew what to do with them. But I was not completely successful and I have come to feel, more and more,
that perhaps I may never be. For I have not yet been able to
discover the purpose of the green motors, in the same room,
or the reason for the mill wheel I saw in the lowlands at the
southern tip of the island (it is connected to the basement by
an iron pipeline, and if it were not so far from the coast I
should imagine it had something to do with the tides; could
it possibly charge the storage batteries of the power plant?).
My ineptitude makes me very frugal; I turn on the motors
only when it is absolutely necessary to do so.

But once I had every light in the museum burning all night
long. That was the second time I made discoveries in the
basement.

I was ill. I hoped that I might find a medicine cabinet
somewhere in the museum. There was nothing upstairs, so
I went down to the basement and—that night I forgot my
sickness, I forgot the horrible, nightmarish existence I was
leading. I discovered a secret door, a stairway, a second basement. I entered a many-sided room, like those bomb shelters
I have seen in movies. The walls were covered with strips of
a material that resembled cork, and with slabs of marble,
arranged symmetrically. I took a step: through stone arches
I saw the same room duplicated eight times in eight direc-
tions as if it were reflected in mirrors. Then I heard the sound
of many footsteps—they were all around me, upstairs, downstairs, all through the museum. I took another step: the sounds
faded away, as if they had been muffled. (It reminded me of
the way a snowstorm on the cold highlands of my Venezuela
deadens all the noises within earshot.)

I went upstairs, back to the silence, the lonely sound of
the sea, the quiet movement of the centipedes. I dreaded an
invasion of ghosts or, less likely, an invasion of the police. I
stood behind a curtain for hours, perhaps minutes, irked by

the hiding place I had chosen (I could be seen from the outside; and if I wanted to escape from someone in the room I would have to open a window). Then, mustering my courage, I searched the house, but I was still uneasy, for there was no mistake about it: I had clearly heard myself surrounded by moving footsteps all through the building, at different levels.

Early the next morning I went down to the basement again. The same footsteps seemed to surround me again, some close, others farther away. But this time I understood them. Annoyed, I continued to explore the second basement, intermittently escorted by the diligent swarm of echoes, many dimensions of the same echo. There are nine identical rooms in the second basement, and five others in a lower basement. They appear to be bomb shelters. Who built this place in 1924 or thereabouts? And why did they abandon it? What sort of bombings were they afraid of? And why should men who could plan such a well-constructed building make a shelter like this, which tries one's mental equilibrium: when I sigh, for example, I can hear the echoes of a sigh, both near and faraway, for two or three minutes afterward. And when there are no echoes, the silence is as horrible as that heavy weight that keeps you from running away in dreams.

From my description the attentive reader can obtain a list of more or less startling objects, situations, facts; the most startling of all, of course, is the sudden arrival of the people who are up on the hill as I write. Are these people connected in some way with the ones who lived here in 1924? Did these visitors build the museum, the chapel, the swimming pool? I find it difficult to believe that one of them ever stopped listening to "Tea for Two" or "Valencia" long enough to design this building, which abounds in echoes, but which is bombproof.

One of these people, a woman, sits on the rocks to watch the sunset every afternoon. She wears a bright scarf over her dark curls; she sits with her hands clasped on one knee;

her skin is burnished by prenatal suns; her eyes, her black hair, her bosom make her look like one of the Spanish or gypsy girls in those paintings I detest.

(Although I have been making entries in this diary at regular intervals, I have not had a chance to work on the books that I hope to write as a kind of justification for my shadowy life on this earth. And yet these lines will serve as a precaution, for they will stay the same even if my ideas change. But I must not forget what I now know is true: for my own safety, I must renounce—once and for all—any help from my fellow men.)

I had nothing to hope for. That was not so horrible—and the acceptance of that fact brought me peace of mind. But now the woman has changed all that. And hope is the one thing I must fear.

She watches the sunset every afternoon; from my hiding place I watch her. Yesterday, and again today, I discovered that my nights and days wait for this hour. The woman, with a gypsy's sensuality and a large, bright-colored scarf on her head, is a ridiculous figure. But still I feel (perhaps I only half believe this) that if she looked at me for a moment, spoke to me only once, I would derive from those simple acts the sort of stimulus a man obtains from friends, from relatives, and, most of all, from the woman he loves.

This hope (although it is against my better judgment) must have been whetted by the people who have kept me away from her: the fishermen and the bearded tennis player. Finding her with the latter today annoyed me; of course I am not jealous. But I was not able to see her yesterday either. As I was on my way to the rocks, the people who were fishing there made it impossible for me to come any closer. They did not speak to me, because I ran away before they saw me.

I tried to elude them from above—impossible. Their friends were up there, watching them fish. The sun had already set when I returned: the lonely rocks bore witness to the night.

Perhaps I am leading myself into a blunder that will have dire consequences; perhaps this woman, tempered by so many late afternoon suns, will betray me to the police.

I may be misjudging her; but I cannot forget the power of the law. Those who are in a position to sentence others impose penalties that make us value liberty above all things.

Now, harassed by dirt and whiskers I cannot eradicate, feeling inordinately the weight of my years, I long for the benign presence of this woman, who is undoubtedly beautiful.

I am certain that the greatest difficulty of all will be to survive her first impression of me. But surely she will not judge me by my appearance alone.

There were three large floods in the past two weeks. Yesterday I almost drowned. The water catches me off guard. I studied the marks on the tree, and calculated the tide for today. But if I had been asleep early this morning I would be dead now. The water rose swiftly with that unusual intensity it has once a week. I cannot account for these surprises; they may be due to mistakes in my calculations, or to a temporary change in the schedule of the high tides. If the tides are always subject to such variations, life in this area will be even more precarious. But I shall survive it. After all, I have been through so much already!

I was sick, in pain, feverish, for a long time; very busy trying not to die of hunger; unable to write (and hating my fellow men).

When I arrived at the island, I found some provisions in the storeroom of the museum. In a very old, charred oven I made an inedible bread of flour, salt, and water. Before very long I was eating flour out of the sack (with sips of water). I used everything that was there, including some spoiled lamb tongues. I used up the matches, allowing myself just three a day. (I feel the deepest respect for the men who first learned how to kindle fires; how much more advanced they were than we!) I had to work for many days, lacerating myself in the process, in an effort to make a trap. When I finally succeeded, I was able to add fresh, bloody birds to my diet. I have followed the tradition of recluses: I have also eaten roots. I learned to recognize the most poisonous plants by the pain I suffered, the attacks of fever, the dreadful discoloration of my skin, the seizures that obliterated my memory, and the unforgettable fears that filled my dreams.[2]

I am miserable. I have no tools down here. This region is unhealthy, sinister. But a few months ago the mere thought of a life like this would have seemed too good to be true.

The daily tides are neither dangerous nor punctual. Sometimes they lift the leafy branches I sleep upon, and I wake up in a mixture of sea water and the muddy water of the marshes.

I hunt during the afternoons; in the morning the water is up to my waist, and the submerged part of my body feels so large and heavy that I can scarcely move. In compensation for these discomforts, there are fewer snakes and lizards. But the mosquitoes are present the whole day, the whole year long.

The tools are in the museum. I hope to be brave enough to try to go and get them later. But that may not be necessary after all—perhaps these people will disappear; perhaps they are merely hallucinations.

The boat, on the beach at the eastern part of the island, is inaccessible now. But my loss of it is not important; all I have really lost is the satisfaction of knowing that I am not a captive, that I can leave the island if I wish to. But was I ever really able to leave? That boat has been a kind of inferno to

---

2. He must have been living under coconut trees. Why, then, does he not mention them? Is it possible he did not see them? Or is it more probable that, since they were diseased, the trees did not produce fruit? (Editor's Note.)

me. When I came here all the way from Rabaul, I had no drinking water, no covering for my head. The sea is endless when you are in a rowboat. I was overwhelmed by the sun, by fatigue. I was plagued by a burning sensation and by dreams that never ceased.

Now I spend my days trying to distinguish the edible roots. I have come to manage my life so well that I do all my work and still have time to rest. This makes me feel free, happy.

Yesterday I lagged behind; today I worked continuously; still there is more work left for tomorrow. When there is so much to do, I do not have time to think about the woman who watches the sunsets.

Yesterday morning the sea invaded the sandbanks. I never saw a tide of such proportions. It was still rising when the rain started (the rains here are infrequent, very heavy, and accompanied by strong winds). I had to find shelter.

I climbed the hill in spite of the odds against me: the slippery terrain, the intense downpour, the strong wind, and the dense foliage. I thought that perhaps I could hide in the chapel (it is the most unfrequented place on the island).

I was in one of the anterooms where the priests eat breakfast and change their clothes (I have not seen a member of the clergy among the occupants of the museum), and all at once two people were standing there, as if they had not arrived, as if they had appeared only in my sight or my imagination. I hid—nervously, stupidly—under the altar, among the red silks and laces. They did not see me. I am still amazed at that.

Even after they had gone I kept on crouching there uncomfortably, frozen, peering cautiously between the silk curtains beneath the main altar, concentrating on the sounds of the storm, watching the dark mountains of the anthills, the undulant paths of large, pale ants, the agitation on the tile floor. I listened to the rain pelting against the walls and the roof, the water stirring in the eaves, the rain pouring on the path outside, the thunder. I could hear the confused sounds of the storm, the rustling trees, the pounding surf resounding on the shore, and I strained my ears to isolate the steps or the voices of someone who might be approaching my hiding place, for I did not want to be taken by surprise again—

I began to hear the fragments of a concise, very faint melody. Then it faded away completely, and I thought of the figures that appear, according to Leonardo, when we look fixedly at damp spots on a wall for any length of time. The music came back; and I listened to it, still crouching, my vision blurred, my body agitated, but thrilled by the beauty of its harmony. In a little while I dared to edge my way over to the window. The water was white on the glass, and opaque, and it was almost impossible to see—I was so taken aback that I was not even afraid to look out through the open door.

The people who live here are dreadful snobs—or else they are the inmates of an abandoned insane asylum! Without any audience (or perhaps their performance has been for my benefit from the beginning), they are enduring discomfort, even risking their lives, in an attempt to be original. And I am not saying this because of my own bitterness: it is the truth. They moved the phonograph out of the green room next to the aquarium, and there they are, men and women together, sitting on benches or sprawling on the ground, chatting, listening to music or dancing, in the midst of a torrential downpour that threatens to uproot all the trees!

———

Now the woman who wears the scarf has become indispensable to me. Perhaps my "no hope" therapy is a little ridiculous; never hope, to avoid disappointment; consider myself dead, to keep from dying. Suddenly I see this feeling as a frightening, disconcerting apathy. I must overcome it. After my escape I managed to live with a kind of indifference to the deadly tedium, and as a result I attained peace of mind. Now I am contemplating a move that may send me back to my past or to the judges; but anything would be preferable to the utter purgatory I am living in.

It all started a week ago. That was when I first observed the miraculous appearance of these people; in the afternoon I stood by the rocks at the western part of the island, trembling. I told myself that all this was vulgar: like any recluse who had been alone too long, I was falling in love with a woman who was nothing but a gypsy. I went back to see her the next afternoon, and the next. She was there, and her presence began to take on the quality of a miracle. After that came the awful days when I did not see her because the fishermen and the bearded man were there; then the flood came, and I tried to protect myself from its devastation. This afternoon—

———

I am afraid. But more than that I am angry at myself. Now I must wait for those people to come and get me at any moment. If there is a delay it can only mean they are setting a trap for me. I shall hide this diary, invent some explanation, and wait for them near the boat, ready to fight, to escape. But I am not so worried about the dangers I am facing—I am most concerned about the mistake I made—it can deprive me of the woman forever.

After I had bathed, and was clean but more unkempt looking than ever (the humidity has that effect on my beard and hair), I went down to see her. This was my plan: I would wait for her by the rocks, and when she arrived I would be watching the sunset. That would change her surprise, her probable suspicion, to curiosity. Our common devotion to the setting sun would make a favorable impression on her. She would ask my name, we would become friends—

It was very late when I arrived. (My lack of punctuality

exasperates me—to think that in the civilized world, in Caracas, I was always late deliberately; that was one of my most personal characteristics!)

I ruined everything. She was watching the sunset, and suddenly I jumped out from behind some boulders. With my hairy face, and standing above her, I must have appeared more hideous than I actually am.

I imagine they will be coming to get me any moment now. I have not prepared an explanation. I am not afraid.

This woman is not just a gypsy. Her aplomb astounded me, for she gave no indication that she had seen me. She did not blink an eye, or make the slightest movement of any kind.

The sun was still above the horizon, hovering as a kind of mirage. I hurried down to the rocks. I saw her: the bright scarf, her hands clasped on one knee, her glance, enlarging my little world. My breathing became uncontrollable. The rocks, the sea, everything seemed tremulous.

As I watched her, I could hear the ocean with its sounds of movement and fatigue close at hand, as if it had moved to my side. My agitation diminished somewhat. And I began to doubt that she could hear my breathing.

Then, while waiting to speak to her, I was reminded of an old psychological law. It was preferable to address her from a high place; that would make her look up to me. The elevation would compensate, at least in part, for my defects.

I climbed higher on the rocks. The effort made me feel weak. Other things that made me weak were:

My haste: I felt obliged to speak to her that very day. If I wanted to keep her from feeling afraid of me—we were in a lonely place and it was growing dark—I could not wait a minute longer.

The sight of her: As if she were posing for an invisible photographer, she surpassed the calm of the sunset. And I did not wish to interrupt that.

Speaking to her would be an alarming experience. I did not even know whether I had any voice left.

I watched her from my hiding place. I was afraid that she would see me, so I came out, perhaps too abruptly. Even so, her composure was not altered; she ignored me, as if I were invisible.

I hesitated no longer. "Please, young lady," I said, "will you please listen to me," but I hoped she would not listen, because I was so excited I had forgotten what I was going to say. The words "young lady" sounded ridiculous on the island. And besides, my sentence was too imperative (combined with my sudden appearance there, the time of day, the solitude).

I persisted: "I realize you may not wish—"

But I find it impossible now to recall exactly what I said. I was almost unconscious. I spoke in a slow, subdued voice with a composure that suggested impropriety. I repeated the words, "young lady." I stopped talking altogether and began to look at the sunset, hoping that the shared vision of that peaceful scene would bring us together. I spoke again. The effort I was making to control myself pitched my voice even lower, and increased the indecency of my tone. After several more minutes of silence, I insisted, I implored, in what was surely a repulsive manner. And finally I became ridiculous. Trembling, almost shouting, I begged her to insult me, to inform against me even, if only she would break the terrible silence.

It was not as if she had not heard me, as if she had not seen me; rather it seemed that her ears were not used for hearing, that her eyes could not see.

She did insult me, in a sense, by showing that she was not afraid of me. Night had fallen when she picked up her basket and walked slowly up the hill.

The men have not come to get me yet. Perhaps they will not come tonight. Perhaps the woman is unusual in this respect, too—she may not have told them about seeing me. It is very dark tonight. I know the island well: I am not afraid of an army, if it tries to find me at night.

———

It has been, again, as if she did not see me. This time I made the mistake of not speaking to her at all.

When the woman came down to the rocks, I was watching the sunset. She stood there for a moment without moving, looking for a place to spread out her blanket. Then she walked toward me. If I had put out my hand, I would have touched her. This possibility horrified me (as if I had almost touched a ghost). There was something frightening in her complete detachment. But when she sat down at my side it seemed she was defying me, trying to show that she no longer ignored my presence.

She took a book out of her basket and sat there reading. I tried to control my nerves.

Then, as she stopped reading and looked up, I thought, "She is going to ask me a question." But the implacable silence continued. I understood the serious implications of not interrupting it; but still, without any obstinacy, for no reason, I remained silent.

Her companions have not come to get me. Perhaps she has not told them about me. Or they may be worried because I know the island so well (and perhaps they send the woman back each day to make me think she is in love with me, to put me off my guard). I am suspicious. But I am sure I can ferret out any scheme, no matter how cunning it may be.

I have found that I usually imagine that things are going to turn out badly. This tendency started about three or four years ago; it is not accidental; but it is annoying. The fact that the woman comes back each day, that she wants to be near me, all this seems to indicate a change that is too good to be true— Perhaps I can forget my beard, my age, and the police who have pursued me for so long—and who, no doubt, are still searching for me stubbornly, like an effective curse. But I must not let myself be too optimistic. As I write these lines, I have an idea that gives me some hope. I do not believe I have insulted the woman, but still it would not do any harm to apologize to her. What does a man usually do on these occasions? He sends flowers, of course. I have a ridiculous plan; but any gift, no matter how trivial, is touching if it is given in the spirit of humility. There are many flowers on the island. When I arrived I saw some of them growing near the swimming pool and the museum. I should be able to make a small garden for her down by the rocks, enlisting nature's help to gain her confidence. Perhaps the results of my efforts will put an end to her silence and her reserve. It will be a poetic maneuver! I have never worked with colors; I know nothing about art. But I am sure I can make a modest effort, which will be pleasing to her.

I got up very early this morning. My plan was so good that I felt it surely would not fail.

I went to gather the flowers, which are most abundant down in the ravines. I picked the ones that were least ugly. (Even the palest flowers have an almost animal vitality!) When I had picked all I could carry and started to arrange them, I saw that they were dead.

I was going to change my plan, but then I remembered that up on the hill, not far from the museum, there is another place where many flowers grow. As it was early in the morning, I felt certain that the people would still be sleeping, so it would be safe to go there.

I picked several of these very small and scabrous flowers. It seemed that they did not have that monstrous urge to die.

Their disadvantages: they are small, and they grow near the museum.

Almost all morning I exposed myself to the danger of being seen by anyone brave enough to get up before ten o'clock. But while I was gathering the flowers, I kept an eye on the museum and did not see any signs of life; this allows me to suppose, to be certain, that I was not observed either.

The flowers are very small. I shall have to plant literally thousands of them if I want my garden to be noticed.

I spent a long time preparing the soil, breaking the ground (it is hard, and I have a large surface to cover), and sprinkling it with rain water. When the ground is ready, I shall have to find more flowers. I shall try to keep those people from seeing me, or from seeing my garden before it is finished. I had almost forgotten that there are cosmic demands on the life of a plant. And after all my work, the risk I have taken, the flowers may not even live until sunset.

I see that I have no artistic talent whatever, but I am sure my garden will be quite touching, between the clumps of grass and hay. Naturally, it will be a fraud. Although it will look like a cultivated garden this afternoon, it will be wilted by tomorrow, or, if there is a wind, it may have no flowers at all.

It rather embarrasses me to reveal the design of my garden. An immense woman is seated, watching the sunset, with her hands clasped on one knee; a diminutive man, made of leaves, kneels in front of the woman (he will be labeled *I*). And underneath it I shall make this inscription:

> Sublime, close at hand but mysterious
> With the living silence of the rose.

My fatigue almost sickens me. I could sleep under the trees until this evening, but I shall not do it. It must be my nerves that make me feel this urge to write. And the reason I am so nervous is that everything I do now is leading me to one of three possible futures: to the woman, to solitude (or the living death in which I spent the past few years, an impossibility now that I have seen the woman), or to a horrible sentence. Which one will it be? Time alone will tell. But still I know that writing this diary can perhaps provide the answer; it may even help produce the right future.

When I made this garden, I felt like a magician because the finished work had no connection with the precise movements that produced it. My magic depended on this: I had to concentrate on each part, on the difficult task of planting each flower and aligning it with the preceding one. As I worked, the garden appeared to be either a disorderly conglomeration of flowers or a woman.

And yet the finished garden is quite beautiful. But I was not able to create it exactly as I had planned. In imagination it is no more difficult to make a woman standing than to make one seated with her hands clasped on one knee; but in reality it is almost impossible to create the latter out of flowers. The woman is shown from the front view, with her head in profile, looking at the sunset. A scarf made of violet-colored flowers covers her head. Her skin is not right. I could not find any flowers of that somber color that repels and attracts me at the same time. Her dress and the ocean are made of blue and of white flowers. The sun is composed of some strange sunflowers that grow on this island. I am shown in profile view, kneeling. I am small (a third of the size of the woman) and green, made of leaves.

I had to modify the inscription. The first one was too long to make out of flowers. I changed it to this:

> You have awakened me from a living death on
> this island.

I liked the idea of calling myself a dead man who suffered from insomnia. I liked it so well, I almost forgot to be

courteous—she might have interpreted the phrase as a re-
proach. But I believe I was blinded by my wish to appear as an
ex-corpse, and I was delighted with the discovery that death
was impossible if I could be with the woman. The variations
with all their monotony were almost monstrous:

You have kept a dead man on this island from sleeping.

or:
I am no longer dead: I am in love.

But I lost my courage. The inscription on the flowers says:

The humble tribute of my love.

The way things turned out was natural enough, but un-
expectedly merciful. I am lost. My little garden was a dreadful mistake. When Ajax—or some other Hellenic name I have
forgotten now—slaughtered the animals, he made a mistake
of equal magnitude; but in this case, I am the slaughtered
animals.

This afternoon the woman came earlier than usual. She
left her book and basket on a rock, and spread out her blanket close to the shore. She was wearing a tennis dress and
a violet-colored head scarf. She sat there for a moment,
watching the sea, as if she were only half awake; then she
stood up and went to get her book. She moved with that freedom we have when we are alone. As she passed my little
garden she pretended not to notice it. I did not mind, for the
moment she arrived I realized what an atrocious failure it
was, and I was miserable because it was too late to do anything about it. When the woman opened her book, put her
fingers between the pages, and continued to watch the sunset, I began to feel less nervous. She did not go away until
night had fallen.

Now I derive consolation from thinking about her disapproval. And I wonder whether it is justified. What is there to hope for after this stupid mistake I have made? But since I can still recognize my own limitations, perhaps she will excuse me. Of course, I was at fault for having created the garden in the first place.

I was going to say that my experiment shows the dangers of creation, the difficulty of balancing more than one consciousness simultaneously. But what good would that do? What solace could I derive from that? Everything is lost now: the woman, my past solitude. Since I cannot escape, I continue with this monologue, which now is unjustifiable.

In spite of my nervousness I felt inspired today when I spent the afternoon sharing the undefiled serenity, the magnificence of the woman. I experienced the same sense of well-being again at night, when I dreamed about the bordello of blind women that Ombrellieri and I visited in Calcutta. In the dream I saw the woman of the sunsets and suddenly the bordello changed into an opulent Florentine palace. I was dazzled by it all, and I heard myself exclaim, "How romantic!" as I sobbed with complacent joy.

But I slept fitfully, remembering that I did not measure up to the woman's strict demands. I shall never be able to forget it: she controlled her distaste and pretended, kindly, not to see my horrible little garden. I was miserable, too, hearing "Tea for Two" and "Valencia," which that blatant phonograph repeated until sunrise.

All that I have written about my life—hopefully or with apprehension, in jest or seriously—mortifies me.

I am in a bad state of mind. It seems that for a long time I have known that everything I do is wrong, and yet I have kept on the same way, stupidly, obstinately. I might have acted this way in a dream, or if I were insane— When I slept this afternoon, I had this dream, like a symbolic and premature commentary on my life: as I was playing a game of croquet, I learned that my part in the game was killing a man. Then, suddenly, I knew I was that man.

Now the nightmare continues. I am a failure, and now I even tell my dreams. I want to wake up, but I am confronted with the sort of resistance that keeps us from freeing ourselves from our most atrocious dreams.

Today the woman was trying to show me her indifference, and she succeeded. But why is she so cruel? Even though I am the victim, I can view the situation objectively.

She was with the dreadful tennis player. His appearance should discourage any feelings of jealousy. He is very tall and was wearing a wine-colored tennis jacket, which was much too large for him, white slacks, and huge yellow and white shoes. His beard seemed to be false, his skin effeminate, waxy, mottled on his temples. His eyes are dark; his teeth, ugly. He speaks slowly, opening his small round mouth wide, vocalizing in a childish way, revealing a small round crimson tongue, which is always close to his lower teeth. His hands are long and pallid—I sense that they are slightly moist.

When I saw them approaching I hid at once. The woman must have seen me; at least, I suppose she did for not once did she look in my direction.

I am quite sure that the man did not notice the little garden until later. And, as before, she pretended not to see it.

They were speaking French. They stood, simply watching the sea, as if something had saddened them. The man said a few words I could not hear. Each time a wave broke against the boulders, I took two or three quick steps in their direction. They were French. The woman shook her head. I did not hear what she said, but it was clearly a negative reply. She closed her eyes and smiled sweetly.

"Please believe me, Faustine—" began the bearded man with obvious desperation, and I found out her name, at last! (Of course, it does not matter now.)

"No— Now I know what you really want—"

She smiled again, with no bitterness or ecstasy, with a certain frivolity. I know that I hated her then. She was just playing with us.

"What a pity that we cannot come to an understanding! We have only a short time left—three days, and then it will all be over."

I do not know what he meant. All I know is that he must be my enemy. He seemed to be sad; but I should not be surprised to learn that this was merely a pose. Faustine's behavior is grotesque; it is almost driving me mad!

The man tried to mitigate the gravity of his statement. He said several sentences that had approximately this meaning: "There's nothing to worry about. We are not going to discuss an eternity—"

"Morel," said Faustine stupidly, "do you know that I find you mysterious?"

In spite of Faustine's questions he remained in his light-hearted mood.

The bearded man went to get her scarf and basket. She had left them on a rock a few feet away. He came back shaking the sand out of them, and said, "Don't take my words so seriously. Sometimes I think that if I am able to arouse your curiosity— But please don't be angry."

When he went to get her things, and then again on the way back, he stepped on my garden. Did he do it deliberately, or did he just not happen to notice it? Faustine saw it, I swear that she did, and yet she would not spare me that insult. She smiled and asked questions with a great show of interest; it was almost as if she surrendered her whole being to him, so complete was her curiosity. But I do not like her attitude. The little garden is no doubt in wretched taste. But why should she stand there calmly and let a disgusting man trample on it? Have I not been trampled on enough already?

But then—what can you expect of people like that? They are the sort you find on indecent postcards. How well they go together: a pale bearded man and a buxom gypsy girl with enormous eyes—I even feel I have seen them in the best collections in Caracas.

And still I wonder: what does all this mean? Certainly she is a detestable person. But what is she after? She may be playing with the bearded man and me; but then again he may be a tool that enables her to tease me. She does not care if she makes him suffer. Perhaps Morel only serves to emphasize her complete repudiation of me, to portend the inevitable climax and the disastrous outcome of this repudiation!

But if not— Oh, it has been such a long time now since she has seen me. I think I shall kill her, or go mad, if this continues any longer. I find myself wondering whether the disease-ridden marshes I have been living in have made me invisible. And, if that were the case, it would be an advantage: then I could seduce Faustine without any danger—

Yesterday I did not visit the rocks. I told myself over and over again that I would not go today either. But by the middle of the afternoon I knew that I had to go. Faustine was not there, and now I am wondering when she will come back. I suppose that her trampling of my garden has brought her fun with me to an end. Now I will bore her like a joke that was amusing once but does not bear repeating. And I will see to it that it is not repeated!

But, as I sat on the rocks waiting, I was miserable. "It's all my fault," I said to myself (that Faustine did not come), "because I was so sure *I* was not coming!"

I climbed the hill, hoping for a glimpse of her. I came out

from behind a clump of bushes, and found myself facing two men and a woman. I stood still, I did not dare to breathe; there was nothing separating us but twenty feet of empty, crepuscular space. The men had their backs to me, but the woman faced them, and she was looking right at me. I saw her shudder. She turned quickly and looked toward the museum. I crouched down behind some bushy plants. I heard her say, "This is not the proper time for ghost stories. We'd better go in now!"

I still do not know whether they were actually telling such stories, or if she mentioned ghosts only to announce a strange occurrence (my presence).

They went away. I saw a man and woman strolling by, not far away. I was afraid they would see me. As they approached, I heard a familiar voice say, "Today I didn't go to see—" (I began to tremble violently. I was sure that she was talking about me.)

"And are you sorry?"

I did not hear Faustine's answer. I noticed that the bearded man had made some progress, because they were using the intimate form of address.

I have come back to the lowlands. I have decided to stay here until the sea carries me away. If the intruders come to get me, I shall not surrender; I shall not try to escape.

My plan not to let Faustine see me again lasted for four days (and was helped by two tides that gave me a lot of work to do).

The fifth day I went to the rocks early. Then I saw Faustine and that damned tennis player. They spoke French correctly, too correctly—like South Americans.

"So you no longer trust me?"

"No."

"But you used to have faith in me—"

There was a coolness between them now. I was reminded of persons who slip back into their old habits of formal speech soon after beginning to speak with intimacy. Their conversation might have made me think of that. But I thought about the idea of a return to the past in a different sense also.

"Would you believe me if I said I could take you back to a time before that afternoon in Vincennes?"

"No, I could never believe you again. Never."

"The influence of the future on the past," said Morel enthusiastically, almost inaudibly.

They stood together, looking at the sea. The man seemed to be trying to break an oppressive tension between them.

"Please believe me, Faustine—"

I remember thinking what a stubborn person he was. He was repeating the same demands I had heard him make the week before.

"No— Now I know what you really want—"

Conversations are subject to repetition, although one cannot explain this phenomenon. I would not have the reader attribute that statement to any bitterness on my part, nor to the very facile association of the words "fugitive," "recluse," "misanthrope." But I gave the matter some study before my trial—conversations are an exchange of news (example: meteorological), of joy or irritation already known or shared by the participants (example: intellectual). But all conversations spring from the pleasure of speaking, from the desire to express agreement and disagreement.

Watching Morel and Faustine, listening to them, I felt that something strange was happening; I did not know what it was. All I knew was that Morel infuriated me.

"If I told you what I really wanted—"

"Would I take offense?"

"No, I think it would help us to understand each other better. We have only a short time left. Three days. What a pity that we cannot come to an understanding!"

I began to realize that the words and movements of Faustine and the bearded man coincided with those of a week ago. The atrocious eternal return. But today one element was missing. My little garden, mutilated by Morel's footsteps, is a mudhole now, with parts of dead flowers crushed into the ground.

I felt elated. I thought I had made this discovery: that there are unexpected, constant repetitions in our behavior. The right combination of circumstances had enabled me to observe them. One seldom has the chance to be a clandestine witness of several talks between the same people. But scenes are repeated in life, just as they are in the theatre.

After hearing Faustine and Morel speak, I turned back to the page (in my diary) where I reported their previous conversation, and I was able to verify that their words and actions were, essentially, the same (the few minor lapses I noticed were due to my own inaccuracy in reporting).

And then I began to suspect angrily that they were merely putting on a comic performance as a joke at my expense.

But let me explain. I never doubted for a minute the importance of trying to make Faustine realize that she and I were all that mattered (and that the bearded man had no place in our plans). I had begun to feel the desire to castigate him in some way—I played with the idea without acting upon it—to insult him by making him look ridiculous to her.

Now I had the chance. But how could I take advantage of it? I found it hard to think because of my anger.

I stood still, pretending to be lost in thought, waiting for the moment when I would be face to face with him. The bearded man went to get Faustine's scarf and basket. He came back shaking the sand out of them, saying (as he had said before): "Don't take my words so seriously. Sometimes I think—"

He was only a few feet away from Faustine. I was not sure what I was going to do. Spontaneity is the mother of crudity. I pointed at the bearded man, as if I were introducing him to Faustine, and shouted, "La femme à barbe, Madame Faustine!"

It was a very bad joke; in fact, it was not even clear whether I was speaking to her or to him.

The bearded man kept on walking toward Faustine, and if I had not moved in time he would have walked right into me. The woman did not stop asking questions; she did not interrupt her look of contentment. Her serenity still appalls me.

Since that moment I have been miserable and ashamed, and I have felt an urge to kneel at Faustine's feet. This afternoon I could not wait until sunset. I went straight to the hill, ready to give myself up, certain that if all went well I would soon be involved in a sentimental scene with Faustine. But I was wrong. There is no explanation for what has happened. *The hill is deserted now!*

When I saw that there was no one on the hill, I was afraid that this was some sort of a trap, that they were really hiding, lying in wait for me. Overcome with dread, I searched the whole museum, exercising extreme caution. But I had only to look at the furniture and the walls, which seemed to be invested with isolation, to be convinced that no one was there. What is more: to be convinced that no one was ever there. It is difficult, after an absence of almost twenty days, to be able to state positively that all the objects in a house with a great many rooms are exactly where they were when one went away; but it seems clear that these fifteen people (and an equal number of servants) did not move a bench, a lamp, or if they did they put everything back in its place, in the exact position it occupied before. I have inspected the kitchen and the laundry room; the meal I left twenty days ago, the clothes (stolen from a closet in the museum) that I hung up to dry twenty days ago, were there; the former spoiled, the latter dry, both untouched.

I shouted in the empty building, "Faustine! Faustine!"

There was no reply.

(I can think of two facts—a fact and a memory—that may be an explanation for these strange occurrences. Recently I started to experiment with new roots. I believe that in Mexico the Indians make a drink from the juice of certain roots, and—if I remember correctly—it causes a person to become delirious for several days. The conclusion, used to explain the presence of Faustine and her friends on this island, is logically admissible; but I do not seriously believe it applies in this case. Now that I have lost Faustine I should like to submit these problems to a hypothetical observer, a third person.)

And then I remembered, incredulously, that I was a fugitive and that justice still had its infernal power. Perhaps these people were playing an outrageous trick on me. If so, I must not give up now, or weaken my powers of resistance, for a horrible catastrophe could result.

I inspected the chapel, the basements. I decided to look at the whole island before going to bed. I went to the rocks, to the grassy part of the hill, to the beaches, the lowlands (my caution was excessive). I had to accept the fact that the intruders were not on the island.

But when I returned to the museum it was almost dark, and I felt nervous. I wanted the brightness of the electric light. I tried many switches; there was no illumination. This seems to confirm my belief that the tides furnish the energy for the motors (by means of that hydraulic mill or water wheel I saw in the lowlands). Those people must have wasted the light. There has been a long period of calm since the last two tides. It ended this very afternoon, when I went back to the museum. I had to close all the doors and windows; I thought that the wind and the sea were going to destroy the island.

In the first basement, standing alongside motors that looked enormous in the shadows, I felt very depressed. The effort needed to kill myself was superfluous now, because with Faustine gone not even the anachronous satisfaction of death remained.

—

To justify my descent into the basement, I tried to make the machinery work. There were a few weak explosions and then everything was quiet again, while outside the storm raged and the branches of the cedar tree scraped against the thick glass of the skylight.

When I came upstairs I heard the hum of a motor; with incredible speed the light touched everything and placed me in front of two men: one in white, the other in green (a cook and a manservant). They were speaking Spanish.

"Do you know why he chose this deserted spot?"

"He must have his reasons!"

I listened anxiously. These were not the same people. These new ghosts were Iberian (did they exist only in my brain, tortured by the privations I had suffered, by the poisonous roots and the equatorial sun, or were they really here on this deadly island?); their words made me conclude that Faustine had not returned.

They continued to converse in low tones, as if they had not heard my footsteps, as if I were not there.

"I don't deny that; but how did Morel happen to think of it in the first place?"

At this point they were interrupted by a man who said angrily, "Say, when are you coming anyway? Dinner has been ready for an hour!"

He stared at them (so intently that I suspected he was trying to resist an urge to look at me), and then ran off shouting excitedly. He was followed by the cook; the servant hurried away in the opposite direction.

I tried hard to control my nerves, but I was trembling. I heard a gong. In a situation like this, anyone, no matter how brave, would have been afraid, and I was no exception. Fortunately, though, I soon remembered that gong. I had seen it many times in the dining room.

I wanted to escape, but I restrained myself, because I knew I could not really run away; that was impossible. The storm, the boat, the night: even if the storm had ended, it would have been horrible to be out at sea on that moonless night. Besides, I was certain that the boat would not be long in capsizing. And surely the lowlands were flooded. If I ran away, where could I go? It would be better to listen; to watch the movements of these people; to wait.

I looked for a place to hide and chose a little room that I found under the stairway. (How stupid! If they had tried to find me, they would have looked there first!) I stayed in my hiding place for a while not daring to think, feeling slightly more relaxed but still bewildered.

Two problems occurred to me:

How did they get to this island? With a storm like this no captain would have dared to approach the shore; it was absurd to imagine that they had transferred to small boats while out at sea, and then used them to land on the island.

When did they come? Their dinner had been ready for a long time; yet when I went down to inspect the motors, less than fifteen minutes ago, there was no one on the island.

They mentioned Morel. Surely, it all had something to do with a return of the same people. It is probable, I thought tremblingly, that I shall have a chance to see Faustine again after all!

I peered out, expecting that someone would be waiting to seize me and then my dilemma would be over.

No one was there.

I went up the stairs and walked along the narrow balcony; then I stood behind one of the terracotta idols, and looked down on the dining room.

About a dozen people were seated at the table. I took them

for a group of tourists from New Zealand or Australia; they appeared to be settled here, as if they did not plan to leave for some time.

I remember it well: I saw the group; I compared these new people with the others who had been here; I discovered that they did not appear to be transients, and only then did I think of Faustine. I searched for her and found her at once. I had a pleasant surprise: the bearded man was not at her side; a precarious joy, which I could scarcely believe: the bearded man was not there (but soon afterward I saw him across the table).

The conversation was not very animated. Morel brought up the subject of immortality. They spoke about travel, parties, diets. Faustine and a blond girl talked about different kinds of medicine. Alec, a young man, whose hair was carefully combed, an Oriental type with green eyes, tried to interest them in the subject of his wool business. He was singularly unsuccessful and soon gave up. Morel waxed enthusiastic about his plans for a ball field or tennis court for the island.

I recognized a few more of the people from the museum. On Faustine's left was a woman—Dora?—with blond curly hair; she smiled frequently, and her large head leaned forward slightly, making me think of a spirited horse. On Faustine's other side there was a dark young man, with bright eyes, bushy hair, and an intense look. Next to him sat a tall, flat-chested, extremely long-armed girl with an expression of disgust. Her name is Irene. On her other side was the woman who said, "This is not the proper time for ghost stories," that night when I was up on the hill. I cannot remember the others.

When I was a little boy, I used to play a game with the pictures in my books: I looked at them for a long time and new objects would keep appearing in an endless succession. Now as I stood there, feeling thwarted, I stared at the panels by Foujita with pictures of women, tigers, or cats.

The people filed into the assembly hall. I left the balcony, feeling terrified, for I knew my enemies were everywhere, including the basement (the servants). I went down the service stairs to the door that was concealed by a screen. The first thing I saw was a woman knitting by one of the alabaster urns and then the woman named Irene, talking to a friend. I looked again, risking the possibility of being seen, and caught a glimpse of Morel at a table with five other people, playing cards. Faustine was sitting there with her back to me. The table was small, their feet were close together, and I stood there for several minutes, perhaps longer than I realized, oblivious to the danger of being observed as I tried to see whether Morel's feet and Faustine's were touching. Then this lamentable pursuit came to an abrupt end; for I saw a red-faced, astonished servant standing there watching me. He turned and went into the assembly hall. I heard footsteps. I hurried away. I hid between the first and second rows of alabaster columns in the round room where the floor was an aquarium. Fish were swimming about beneath my feet; they were identical counterparts of the dead ones I had removed shortly after I arrived on the island.

When I regained my composure, I moved toward the door. Faustine, Dora—her dinner companion—and Alec were coming up the stairs. Faustine walked slowly, with measured steps. As I looked at her I reflected that I was risking everything—my own peace of mind, the Universe, memories, my intense anxiety, the pleasure of learning about the tides and about more than one inoffensive root—for that ample body, those long, slender legs, that ridiculous sensuality.

I followed them. They turned abruptly and entered a room. Across the hall I saw an open door that revealed a lighted, empty room. I entered it cautiously. Apparently the person who had been there had forgotten to turn out the light. The neatness of the bed and of the dressing table, the absence of books and clothes, and the perfect order told me that no one was living in it.

I was uneasy when the other occupants of the museum went to their rooms. I heard their footsteps on the stairs and tried to turn out my light, but it was impossible: the switch did not work. I did not try to fix it, for it occurred to me that a light going off in an empty room would attract attention.

If it had not been for that broken switch perhaps I would have gone to sleep immediately, because I was so tired, and because I saw the lights go out, one by one, through the cracks in the doors down the hall. (I found it reassuring to know that Dora was in Faustine's room!) I could imagine that if anyone happened to walk through the hall he would come into my room to turn out the light (the rest of the museum was in total darkness). Perhaps it was inevitable that someone would enter, but I would not be in any real danger. When he saw that the switch was broken, the person would simply go away to avoid disturbing the others. I would have to hide for only a moment.

I was thinking about this when Dora's head appeared in the doorway. Her eyes looked through me. She went away, without trying to turn out the light.

I felt terrified. Now, my position compromised, I began to explore the building in my imagination, to find a safe hiding place. I did not want to leave that room, for as long as I was there I could guard Faustine's door. I sat down on the bed, leaned back, and went to sleep. Soon afterward I saw Faustine in a dream. She entered the room. She came very close to me. I woke up. The light was out. I tried not to move; I tried to be-gin to see in the darkness, but I could not control my breath-ing and my terror.

I got up, went out into the hall, and heard the silence that had followed the storm: nothing interrupted it.

I started to walk down the hall, feeling that a door would

open suddenly and a pair of rough hands would reach out and grab me, a mocking voice would taunt me. The strange world I had been living in, my conjectures and anxieties, Faustine—they all seemed like an invisible path that was leading me straight to prison and death. I went downstairs, moving cautiously through the darkness. I came to a door and tried to open it, but I could not budge it—I could not even move the latch. (I have seen latches that were stuck before; but I do not understand the windows: they have no locks and yet it is impossible to open them.) I was becoming convinced that I would never be able to get out of there, I was growing more nervous and—perhaps because of this and because of my helplessness in the dark—it seemed that even the doors in the interior of the building were impossible to open. Some footsteps on the service stairs made me hurry. I did not know how to get out of the room. I felt my way along a wall, until I came to one of the enormous alabaster urns; with considerable effort and danger, I slid inside of it.

For a long time I huddled nervously against the slippery alabaster surface and the fragile lamp. I wondered if Faustine had stayed alone with Alec, or if he or she had gone out with Dora when the latter left the room.

This morning I was awakened by the sound of voices (I was very weak and too sleepy to hear what they were saying). Then everything was quiet.

I wanted to get away from the museum. I started to stand up, afraid that I would fall and break the enormous light bulb, or that someone would see my head as it emerged from the urn. Very slowly, laboriously, I climbed out. I hid behind the curtains for a moment. I was so weak that I could not move them; they seemed to be rigid and heavy, like the stone curtains carved on a tomb. I could visualize, painfully, the fancy pastries and other foods that civilization had to offer: I was sure I would find such things in the pantry. I had fainting spells, the urge to laugh out loud; then I walked boldly toward the staircase. The door was open. No one was inside. I went into the pantry—my courage made me proud. I heard footsteps. I tried to open a door to the outside, and again I encountered one of those inexorable latches. Someone was coming down the service stairs. I ran to the entrance to the pantry. Through the open door I could see part of a wicker chair and a pair of crossed legs. I turned toward the main stairway; I heard more footsteps. There were people in the dining room. I went into the assembly hall, noticed an open window, and, almost at the same time, I saw Irene and the woman who had spoken of ghosts, and the young man with the bushy hair; he walked toward me with an open book, reciting French poetry. I stopped short. Then I threaded my way stiffly between those people, almost touching them as I passed; I jumped out of the window and, in spite of the pain that racked my legs (it is about fifteen feet from the window to the ground below), I ran down through the ravine, stumbling and falling as I went, not daring to look back.

I found some food, and began to wolf it down. Suddenly I stopped, for I had lost my appetite.

Now my pain is almost gone. I am more serene. I think, although I know it seems absurd, that perhaps they did not see me in the museum. The whole day has gone by and no one has come to get me. It is frightening to accept so much good fortune!

Here is some evidence that can help my readers establish the date of the intruders' second appearance here: the following day two moons and two suns were visible, possibly only a local phenomenon; but probably they are a kind of mirage, caused by the moon or the sun, the sea and the air, and are surely visible from Rabaul and throughout this whole area. I noticed that the second sun—perhaps a reflection of the other—is much more intense. It seems that the temperature has risen infernally during the past two days, as if the new sun brought with it an unbearably hot summer. The nights are very white: there is a kind of polar glare in the air. But I imagine that the two moons and two suns hold no special interest now, for they must have been noted everywhere, either in the sky itself or in detailed and scholarly reports. I am not mentioning them because of any poetic attachment, or because of their rarity, but rather to give my readers, who receive newspapers and celebrate birthdays, a way to date these pages.

As far as I know, these are the first nights when two moons have been observed. But two suns were seen once before. Cicero speaks of them in *De Natura Deorum*: "Tum sole quod ut e patre audivi Tuditano et Aquilio consulibus evenerat."

I believe that is the correct version of the quotation.[3] At the Miranda Institute, M. Lobre made us memorize the first five pages of the Second Book and the last three pages of the Third Book. That is all I know about *The Nature of the Gods*.

The intruders did not come to get me. I can see them come and go on the hillside. Perhaps some imperfection in my soul (and the infinite numbers of mosquitoes) caused me to long for last night, when I had lost all hope of finding Faustine, and I did not feel this bitter anguish. Now I miss that moment when I thought I was settled once again in the museum, the undisputed master of my solitude.

I remember what it was I was thinking about the night before last, in that insistently lighted room: About the nature of the intruders, about my relationship with them.

I tried several explanations.

I may have the famous disease that is associated with this

---

3. He is mistaken. He omits the most important word: *geminato* (from *geminatus*: "coupled, duplicated, repeated, reiterated"). The phrase is: "... tum sole geminato, quod, ut e patre audivi, Tuditano et Aquilio consulibus evenerat; quo quidem anno P. Africanus sol alter extinctus est." Translation: The two suns that, as I heard from my father, were seen in the Consulate of Tuditanus and Aquilius, in the year (183 B.C.) when the sun of Publius Africanus was extinguished. (Editor's Note.)

island; it may have caused me to imagine the people, the music, Faustine; perhaps my body has developed horrible lesions, the signs of approaching death, which the other effects keep me from noticing.

The polluted air of the lowlands and my improper diet may have made me invisible. The intruders did not see me. (Else they have a superhuman discipline. I discarded secretly, with the certainty that I am right, my suspicion that this is a plot organized by the police to capture me.) Objection: I am not invisible to the birds, the lizards, the rats, the mosquitoes.

It occurred to me (precariously) that these could be beings from another planet, whose nature is different from ours, with eyes that are not used for seeing, with ears that do not hear. I remembered that they spoke correct French. I enlarged the foregoing monstrosity: this language may be a parallel attribute of our worlds, but the words may have different meanings!

I arrived at the fourth theory because of my mad impulse to relate my dreams. This is what I dreamed last night:

I was in an insane asylum. After a long consultation with a doctor (the trial?), my family had me taken there. Morel was the director of the asylum. Sometimes I knew I was on the island; sometimes I thought I was in the insane asylum; sometimes I was the director of the insane asylum.

I do not believe that a dream should necessarily be taken for reality, or reality for madness.

Fifth hypothesis: the intruders are a group of dead friends, and I am a traveler, like Dante or Swedenborg, or some other dead man of another sort, at a different phase of his metamorphosis; this island may be the purgatory or the heaven of those dead people (the possibility of several heavens has already been suggested; if only one existed, and if everyone went there and found a happy marriage and literary meetings on Wednesdays, many of us would have stopped dying).

Now I understand why novelists write about ghosts that weep and wail. The dead remain in the midst of the living. It is hard for them, after all, to change their habits—to give up smoking, or the prestige of being great lovers. I was horrified by the thought that I was invisible; horrified that Faustine, who was so close to me, actually might be on another planet (the sound of her name made me sad); but I am dead, I am out of reach, I thought; and I shall see Faustine, I shall see her go away, but my gestures, my pleas, my efforts will have no effect on her. And I knew that those horrible solutions were nothing but frustrated hopes.

Thinking about these ideas left me in a state of euphoria. I had proof that my relationship with the intruders was a relationship between beings on different planes. There could have been some catastrophe on the island that was imperceptible for its dead (I and the animals), after which the intruders arrived.

So I was dead! The thought delighted me. (I felt proud, I felt as if I were a character in a novel!)

I thought about my life. My unexciting childhood, the afternoons I spent on Paradise Street in Caracas; the days before my arrest—it seemed as if someone else had lived them; my long escape from justice; the months I have been living on this island. On two occasions I very nearly died. Once, when I was in my room at the fetid rose-colored boarding-house at 11 West Street, during the days before the police came to get me (if I had died then, the trial would have been before the definitive Judge; my escape and my travels would have been the journey to heaven, hell, or purgatory). The other time was during the boat trip. The sun was melting my cranium and, although I rowed all the way to the island, I must have lost consciousness long before I arrived. All the memories of those days are imprecise; the only things I can recall are an infernal light, a constant swaying and the sound of water, a pain far greater than all our capacity for suffering.

I had been thinking about all this for a long time, so now I was quite tired, and I continued less logically: I was not dead until the intruders arrived; when one is alone it is impossible to be dead. Now I must eliminate the witnesses before I can come back to life. That will not be difficult: I do not exist, and therefore they will not suspect their own destruction.

And I had another idea, an incredible plan for a very private seduction, which, like a dream, would exist only for me.

These vain and unjustifiable explanations came to me during moments of extreme anxiety. But men and love-making cannot endure prolonged intensity.

I think I must be in hell. The two suns are unbearable. I am not feeling well, either, because of something I ate: some very fibrous bulbs that looked like turnips.

The suns were overhead, one above the other, and suddenly (I believe I was watching the sea until that moment) a ship loomed up very close, between the reefs. It was as if I had been sleeping (even the flies move about in their sleep, under this double sun!) and had awakened, seconds or hours later, without noticing that I had been asleep or that I was awakening. The ship was a large white freighter. "The police," I thought with irritation. "They must be coming to search the island." The ship's whistle blew three times. The intruders assembled on the hillside. Some of the women waved handkerchiefs.

The sea was calm. A launch was lowered, but it took the men almost an hour to get the motor started. A man dressed as an officer—perhaps he was the captain—got off on the island. The others returned to the ship.

The man walked up the hill. I was very curious and, in spite of my pains and the indigestible bulbs I had eaten, I

went up on the other side. I saw him salute respectfully. The intruders asked him about his trip, and expressed interest in knowing whether he had "obtained everything" in Rabaul. I was behind a statue of a dying phoenix, unafraid of being seen (it seemed useless to hide). Morel escorted the man to a bench, and they both sat down.

Then I understood why the ship had come. It must have belonged to them, and now it was going to take them away.

I have three choices, I thought. Either to abduct her, to go on board the ship, or to let them take her away from me.

But if I abduct her they will surely send out a search party, and sooner or later they will find us. Is there no place on this whole island where I can hide her?

It also occurred to me that I could take her out of her room at night when everyone was sleeping, and then the two of us would go away together in the small boat. But where would we go? Would the miracle of my trip to the island be repeated? How could I know where to go? Would risking my chances with Faustine make it worth while to hazard the tremendous dangers we would surely encounter in the middle of the ocean? Or perhaps those difficulties would be only too brief: possibly we would sink a few feet from shore.

If I managed to board the ship, without doubt I would be found. Perhaps I could talk to them, ask them to call Faustine or Morel, and then explain everything. I might have time—if they reacted unfavorably to my story—to kill myself before we arrived at the first port where there was a prison.

"I have to make a decision," I thought.

A tall, robust man with a red face, an unkempt black beard, and effeminate mannerisms approached Morel and said, "It's quite late. We still have to get ready, you know."

Morel replied, "Yes, yes. Just wait a moment, please."

The captain stood up. Morel kept on talking with a sense of urgency, patting him on the back several times, and then turned toward the fat man, while the captain saluted, and asked, "Shall we go now?"

The fat man turned to the dark-haired, intense youth who was with him, and repeated, "Shall we go?"

The young man nodded assent.

The three hurried toward the museum, paying no attention to the ladies, who were grouped nearby. The captain walked over to them, smiling courteously, and slowly escorted them in the direction of the museum.

I did not know what to do. Although it was a ridiculous scene, it alarmed me. What were they getting ready for? But still I thought that if I saw them leaving with Faustine, I would not interfere with their horrible plan, but would remain as an inactive, only slightly nervous spectator.

Fortunately, though, it was not yet time. I could see Morel's beard and his thin legs in the distance. Faustine, Dora, the woman who once spoke of ghosts, Alec, and the three men who had been there a short time before were walking down to the pool, in bathing suits. I ran from one clump of plants to another, trying to get a better look. The women hurried along, smiling; the men were engaging in calisthenics, as if they were trying to keep warm—this was inconceivable with two suns overhead. I could imagine how disillusioned they would be when they saw the pool. Since I have stopped changing the water it has become impenetrable (at least for a normal person): green, opaque, slimy, with large clusters of leaves that have grown monstrously, dead birds, and—of course—live snakes and frogs.

Undressed, Faustine is infinitely beautiful. She had that rather foolish abandon people often have when they bathe in public, and she was the first one to dive into the water. I heard them laughing and splashing about gaily.

Dora and the older woman came out first. The latter, waving her arm up and down, counted, "One, two, three!"

They must have been racing. The men came out of the pool, appearing to be exhausted. Faustine stayed in the water a while longer.

In the meantime some of the ship's crew had come over to the island. Now they were walking around. I hid behind some palm trees.

———

I am going to relate exactly what I saw happen from yesterday afternoon to this morning, even though these events are incredible and defy reality. Now it seems that the real situation is not the one I described on the foregoing pages; the situation I am living is not what I think it is.

When the swimmers went to get dressed, I resolved to be on my guard both day and night. However, I soon decided that this would not be necessary.

I was walking away when the dark, intense young man appeared again. A minute later I took Morel by surprise; he was looking through a window, apparently spying on someone. Morel went down the garden steps. I was not far away, and I could hear the conversation.

"I did not want to say anything about this when the others were here. I have something to suggest to you and a few of the others."

"Oh, yes?"

"Not here," said Morel, staring suspiciously at the trees. "Tonight. When everyone has gone, please stay a few minutes longer."

"Even if it is very late?"

"So much the better. The later the better. But above all, be discreet. I don't want the women to find out. Hysterics annoy me. See you later!"

He hurried away. Before he went into the house, he looked back over his shoulder. The boy was going upstairs. A signal from Morel made him stop. He walked back and forth, with his hands in his pockets, whistling naively.

I tried to think about what I had just seen, but I did not want to. It unnerved me.

About fifteen minutes later another bearded man, stout and with grayish hair (I have not yet mentioned him in my diary), appeared on the stairs and stood there looking toward the horizon. He walked down to the museum, seeming to be confused.

Morel came back. They spoke together for a moment. I managed to hear Morel say: "... if I told you that all your words and actions are being recorded?"

"It wouldn't bother me in the slightest."

I wondered if possibly they had found my diary. I was determined to be on the alert, to avoid the temptations of fatigue and distraction, not to let myself be taken by surprise.

The stout man was alone again, and seemed to be bewildered. Morel came back with Alec (the young man with green eyes). The three of them walked away together.

Then I saw some of the men and their servants come out carrying wicker chairs, which they put in the shadow of a large, diseased breadfruit tree (I have seen trees of the same type, only smaller, on an old plantation in Los Teques). The ladies sat down in the chairs; the men sprawled on the grass at their feet. It made me think of afternoons in my own country.

Faustine walked by on her way to the rocks. My love for this woman has become annoying (and ridiculous: we have never even spoken to each other!). She was wearing a tennis dress and that violet-colored scarf on her head. How I shall remember this scarf after Faustine has gone away!

I wanted to offer to carry her basket or her blanket. I followed her at a distance; I saw her leave her basket by a rock, put down her blanket, stand motionless contemplating the sea or the sunset, imposing her calm on both.

This was my last chance with Faustine—my last chance to kneel down, to tell her of my love, my life. But I did nothing. It did not seem right, somehow. True, women naturally welcome any sort of tribute. But in this case it would be better to let the situation develop naturally. We are suspicious of a stranger who tells us his life story, who tells us spontaneously that he has been captured, sentenced to life imprisonment, and that we are his reason for living. We are afraid that he is merely tricking us into buying a fountain pen or a bottle with a miniature sailing vessel inside.

An alternative was to speak to her as I was watching the sea, like a serious, stupid lunatic; to comment on the two suns, on our mutual liking for sunsets; to pause so that she could ask me some questions; to tell her, at least, that I am a writer who has always wanted to live on a lonely island; to confess that I was annoyed when her friends came; to explain that I have been forced to remain on the part of the island which is nearly always flooded (this would lead us into a pleasant discussion of the lowlands and their disasters); and to declare my love and my fears that she is going to leave, that the afternoons will come and go without bringing me the accustomed joy of seeing her.

She stood up. I felt very nervous (as if Faustine had heard what I was thinking and had been offended). She went to get a book from her basket on another rock about fifteen feet away, and sat down again. She opened the book, put her hand on a page, and then looked up, staring at the sunset, as if she were only half awake.

When the weaker of the two suns had set, Faustine stood up again. I followed her. I ran after her and threw myself at her feet and I said, I almost shouted, "Faustine, I love you!"

I thought that if I acted on impulse, she could not doubt my sincerity. I do not know what effect my words had on her,

for I was driven away by some footsteps and a dark shadow. I hid behind a palm tree. My breathing, which was very irregular, almost deafened me.

I heard Morel telling Faustine that he had to talk to her. She replied, "All right—let's go to the museum." (I heard this clearly.)

There was an argument. Morel objected, "No, I want to make the most of this opportunity—away from the museum so our friends will not be able to see us."

I also heard him say: "I am warning you—you are a different kind of woman—you must control your nerves."

I can state categorically that Faustine stubbornly refused to go away with him.

Morel said in a commanding tone, "When everyone else has gone tonight, you are to stay a little longer."

They were walking between the palm trees and the museum. Morel was talkative, and he made many gestures. At one point he took Faustine's arm. Then they walked on in silence. When I saw them enter the museum I decided to find myself some food so I would be feeling well during the night and be able to keep watch.

———

"Tea for Two" and "Valencia" persisted until after dawn. In spite of my plans, I ate very little. The people who were dancing up on the hillside, the viscous leaves, the roots that tasted of the earth, the hard, fibrous bulbs—all these were enough to convince me that I should enter the museum and look for some bread and other real food.

I went in through the coalbin around midnight. There were servants in the pantry and the storeroom. I decided it would be better to hide, to wait until the people went to their rooms. Perhaps I would be able to hear what Morel was going to propose to Faustine, the bushy-haired youth, the fat man, and green-eyed Alec. Then I would steal some food and find a way to get away from there.

It did not really matter very much to me what Morel was going to say. But I was disturbed by the arrival of the ship, and Faustine's imminent, irremediable departure.

As I walked through the large assembly hall, I saw a ghost-copy of the book by Bélidor that I had taken two weeks earlier; it was on the same shelf of green marble, in exactly the same place on the shelf. I felt my pocket; I took out the book. I compared the two: they were not two copies of the same book, but the same copy twice; the light-blue ink on both was blurred, making the word *Perse* indistinct; both had a crooked tear in the lower corner. I am speaking of an external identity—I could not even touch the book on the table. I hurried away, so they would not see me (first, some of the women; then, Morel). I walked through the room with the aquarium floor and hid in the green room, behind the screen of mirrors. Through a crack I could see the room with the aquarium.

Morel was giving orders.

"Put a chair and table here."

They put the other chairs in rows, in front of the table, as if there was going to be a lecture.

When it was very late almost everyone had arrived. There was some commotion, some curiosity, a few smiles; mostly there was an air of fatigued resignation.

"No one has permission to be absent," said Morel. "I shall not begin until everyone is here."

"Jane is not here."

"Jane Gray is not here."

"What's the difference?"

"Someone will have to go and get her."

"But she's in bed!"

"She cannot be absent."

"But she's sleeping!"

"I shall not begin until I see that she is here."

"I'll go and get her," said Dora.

"I'll go with you," said the bushy-haired youth.

I tried to write down the above conversation exactly as it occurred. If it does not seem natural now, either art or my memory is to blame. It seemed natural enough then. Seeing those people, hearing them talk, no one could expect the magical occurrence or the negation of reality that came afterward (although it happened near an illuminated aquarium, on top of long-tailed fish and lichens, in a forest of black pillars!).

Morel was speaking: "You must search the whole building. I saw him enter this room some time ago."

Was he referring to me? At last I was going to find out the real reason why these people had come to the island.

"We've searched the whole house," said a naive voice.

"That doesn't matter. You must find him!" replied Morel.

I felt as if I were surrounded now. I wanted to get away, but I did not dare to move.

I remembered that halls of mirrors were famous as places of torture. I was beginning to feel uncomfortable.

Then Dora and the youth returned with an elderly lady who appeared to be drunk (I had seen her in the pool). Two men, apparently servants, offered to help; they came up to Morel, and one said, "Haven't been able to find him."

"Haynes is sleeping in Faustine's room," said Dora to Morel. "It will be hard to get him down to the meeting."

Was Haynes the one they had been speaking about before? At first I did not see any connection between Dora's remark and Morel's conversation with the men. The latter spoke about looking for someone, and I had felt panic-stricken, finding allusions or threats in everything. Now it occurs to me that these people were never concerned with me at all. Now I know they cannot look for me.

Can I be sure? A sensible man—would he believe what I heard last night, what I believe I know? Would he tell me to forget the nightmare of thinking that all this is a trap set to capture me?

And, if it is a trap, why is it such a complex one? Why do they not simply arrest me? I find this laborious method quite idiotic.

The habits of our lives make us presume that things will happen in a certain foreseeable way, that there will be a vague coherence in the world. Now reality appears to be changed, unreal. When a man awakens, or dies, he is slow to free himself from the terrors of the dream, from the worries and manias of life. Now it will be hard for me to break the habit of being afraid of these people.

Morel took a sheaf of yellow papers filled with typed copy from a wooden bowl on the table. The bowl also contained a number of letters attached to clippings of advertisements from *Yachting* and *Motor Boating*. The letters asked about prices of used boats, terms of sale, addresses where they could be seen. I saw a few of them.

"Let Haynes sleep," said Morel. "He weighs so much—if they try to bring him down, we shall never get started!"

Morel motioned for silence, and then began tentatively, "I have something important to tell you."

He smiled nervously.

"It is nothing to worry about. In the interest of accuracy I have decided to read my speech. Please listen carefully."

(He began to read the yellow pages that I am putting into this envelope. When I ran away from the museum this morning, they were on the table; I took them with me.)[4]

---

4. For the sake of clarity we have enclosed the material on the yellow pages in quotation marks; the marginal notes, written in pencil and in the same handwriting as the rest of the diary, are not set off by quotes. (Editor's Note.)

"You must forgive me for this rather tedious, unpleasant incident. We shall try to forget it! Thoughts of the fine week we have spent here together will make all this seem less important.

"At first, I decided not to tell you anything. That would have spared you a very natural anxiety. We would have enjoyed ourselves up to the very last instant, and there would have been no objections. But, as all of you are friends, you have a right to know."

He paused for a moment, rolling his eyes, smiling, trembling; then he continued impulsively: "My abuse consists of having photographed you without your permission. Of course, it is not like an ordinary photograph; this is my latest invention. We shall live in this photograph forever. Imagine a stage on which our life during these seven days is acted out, complete in every detail. We are the actors. All our actions have been recorded."

"How shameful!" blurted a man with a black moustache and protruding teeth.

"I hope it's just a joke," said Dora.

Faustine was not smiling. She seemed to be indignant.

Morel continued, "I could have told you when we arrived: 'We shall live for eternity.' Perhaps then we would have forced ourselves to maintain a constant gaiety, and that would have ruined everything. I thought: 'Any week we spend together, even if we do not feel obliged to use our time profitably, will be pleasant.' And wasn't it?" He paused. "Well, then, I have given you a pleasant eternity!

"To be sure, nothing created by man is perfect. Some of our friends are missing—it could not be helped. Claude has been excused; he was working on the theory, in the form of a novel with theological overtones, that man and God are at odds with one another; he thinks it will bring him immortality and therefore he does not wish to interrupt his work. For two years now Madeleine has not been going to the mountains; her health has been poor. Leclerc had already arranged to go to Florida with the Davies."

As an afterthought, he added, "Poor Charlie, of course—"

From his tone, which emphasized the word *poor*, from the mute solemnity and the changes of position and the nervous moving of chairs that occurred at once, I inferred that the man named Charlie had died; more precisely, that he had died recently.

Then, as if to reassure his audience, Morel said, "But I have him! If anyone would like to see him, I can show him to you. He was one of my first successful experiments."

He stopped talking as he appeared to perceive the change in the room. The audience had proceeded from an affable boredom to sadness, with a slight reproof for the bad taste of mentioning a deceased friend in a light-hearted recitation; now the people seemed perplexed, almost horrified.

Morel quickly turned back to his yellow papers.

"For a long time now my brain has had two principal occupations: thinking of my inventions and thinking about—" The sympathy between Morel and his audience was definitely re-established.

"For example, as I open the pages of a book, or walk, or fill my pipe, I am imagining a happy life with—"

His words were greeted with bursts of applause.

"When I finished my invention it occurred to me, first as a mere exercise for the imagination, then as an incredible plan, that I could give perpetual reality to my romantic desire.

"My belief in my own superiority and the conviction that it is easier to make a woman fall in love with me than to manufacture heavens made me choose a spontaneous approach. My hopes of making her love me have receded now; I no longer have her confidence; nor do I have the desire, the will, to face life.

"I had to employ certain tactics, make plans." (Morel changed the wording of the sentence to mitigate the serious implications.) "At first I wanted to convince her that she should come here alone with me—but that was impossible: I have not seen her alone since I told her of my love—or else to abduct her; but we would have been fighting eternally! Please note, by the way, that the word *eternally* is not an exaggeration."

There was a considerable stir in the audience. He was saying—it seemed to me—that he had planned to seduce her, and he was trying to be funny.

"Now I shall explain my invention."

———

Up to this point it was a repugnant and badly organized speech. Morel is a scientist, and he becomes more precise when he overlooks his personal feelings and concentrates on his own special field; then his style is still unpleasant, filled with technical words and vain attempts to achieve a certain oratorical force, but at least it is clearer. The reader can judge for himself:

"What is the purpose of radio? To supply food, as it were, for the sense of hearing: by utilizing transmitters and receivers, we can take part in a conversation with Madeleine right in this room, even though she is thousands of miles away in a suburb of Quebec. Television does the same thing for the sense of sight. By achieving slower or faster vibrations, we can apply this principle to the other senses, to all the other senses.

"Until recently, the scientific processes for the different senses were as follows:

"For sight: television, motion pictures, photography.

"For hearing: radio, the phonograph, the telephone.[5]

---

5. The omission of the telegraph seems to be deliberate. Morel is the author of the pamphlet *Que nous envoie Dieu?* (the words of the first telegraphic message sent by Morse); and his reply to this question is: "Un peintre inutile et une invention indiscrète." Nevertheless, paintings like *Lafayette* and the *Dying Hercules* have an undisputed value. (Editor's Note.)

"Conclusion:

"Until recently science had been able to satisfy only the senses of sight and hearing, to compensate for spatial and temporal absences. The first part of my work was valuable because it interrupted an inactivity along these lines that had become traditional, and because it continued, logically and along almost parallel lines, the thought and teachings of the brilliant men who made the world a better place by the inventions I have just mentioned.

"I should like to express my gratitude to the companies that, in France (Société Clunie) and in Switzerland (Schwachter, of Saint Gallen), realized the importance of my research and put their excellent laboratories at my disposal.

"Unfortunately, I cannot say the same of my colleagues.

"When I went to Holland to consult with the distinguished electrical engineer, Jan Van Heuse, the inventor of a primitive lie-detector, I found some encouragement and, I must add, a regrettable attitude of suspicion.

"Since then I have preferred to work alone.

"I began to search for waves and vibrations that had previously been unattainable, to devise instruments to receive and transmit them. I obtained, with relative facility, the olfactory sensations; the so-called thermal and tactile ones required all my perseverance.

"It was also necessary to perfect the existing methods. My best results were a tribute to the manufacturers of phonograph records. For a long time now we have been able to state that we need have no fear of death, at least with regard to the human voice. Photography and motion pictures have made it possible to retain images, although imperfectly. I directed this part of my work toward the retention of the images that appear in mirrors.

"With my machine a person or an animal or a thing is like the station that broadcasts the concert you hear on the radio. If you turn the dial for the olfactory waves, you will smell the jasmine perfume on Madeleine's throat, without seeing her. By turning the dial of the tactile waves, you will be able to stroke her soft, invisible hair and learn, like the blind, to know things by your hands. But if you turn all the dials at once, Madeleine will be reproduced completely, and she will appear exactly as she is; you must not forget that I am speaking of images extracted from mirrors, with the sounds, tactile sensations, flavors, odors, temperatures, all synchronized perfectly. An observer will not realize that they are images. And if our images were to appear now, you yourselves would not believe me. Instead, you would find it easier to think that I had engaged a group of actors, improbable doubles for each of you!

"This is the first part of the machine; the second part makes recordings; the third is a projector. No screens or papers are needed; the projections can be received through space, and it does not matter whether it is day or night. To explain this more clearly, I shall attempt to compare the parts of my machine with the television set that shows the images from more or less distant transmitters; with the camera that takes a motion picture of the images transmitted by the television set; and with the motion-picture projector.

"I thought I would synchronize all the parts of my machine and take scenes of our lives: an afternoon with Faustine, conversations with some of you; and in that way I would be able to make an album of very durable and clear images, which would be a legacy from the present to the future; they would please your children and friends, and the coming generations whose customs will differ from our own.

"I reasoned that if the reproductions of objects would be objects—as a photograph of a house is an object that represents another object—the reproductions of animals and plants would not be animals or plants. I was certain that my images of persons would lack consciousness of themselves (like the characters in a motion picture).

"But I found, to my surprise, that when I succeeded in synchronizing the different parts of the machine, after much hard work, I obtained reconstituted persons who would disappear if I disconnected the projecting apparatus, and would live only the moments when the scene was taken; when the scene ended they would repeat these same moments again and again, like a phonograph record or a motion picture that would end and begin again; moreover, no one could distinguish them from living persons (they appear to be circulating in another world with which our own has made a chance encounter). If we grant consciousness, and all that distinguishes us from objects, to the persons who surround us, we shall have no valid reason to deny it to the persons created by my machinery.

"When all the senses are synchronized, the soul emerges. That was to be expected. When Madeleine existed for the senses of sight, hearing, taste, smell, and touch, Madeleine herself was actually there."

I have shown that Morel's style is unpleasant, with a liberal sprinkling of technical terms, and that it attempts, vainly, to achieve a certain grandiloquence. Its banality is obvious:

"Is it hard for you to accept such a mechanical and artificial system for the reproduction of life? It might help if you bear in mind that what changes the sleight-of-hand artist's movements into magic is our inability to see!

"To make living reproductions, I need living transmitters. I do not create life.

"The thing that is latent in a phonograph record, the thing that is revealed when I press a button and turn on the machine —shouldn't we call that 'life'? Shall I insist, like the mandarins of China, that every life depends on a button which an unknown being can press? And you yourselves—how many times have you wondered about mankind's destiny, or asked the old questions: 'Where are we going? Like the unheard music that lies latent in a phonograph record, where are we until

God orders us to be born?' Don't you see that there is a parallelism between the destinies of men and images?

"The theory that the images have souls seems to be confirmed by the effects of my machine on persons, animals, and vegetables used as transmitters.

"Of course, I did not achieve these results until after many partial reverses. I remember that I made the first tests with employees of the Schwachter Company. With no advance warning, I turned on the machine and took them while they were working. There were still some minor defects in the receiver; it did not assemble their data evenly; in some, for example, the image did not coincide with the tactile sensations; there are times when the errors are imperceptible for unspecialized observers, but occasionally the deviation is broad."

"Can you show us those first images?" asked Stoever.

"If you wish, of course; but I warn you that some of the ghosts are slightly monstrous!" replied Morel.

"Very well," said Dora. "Show them to us. A little entertainment is always welcome."

"I want to see them," continued Stoever, "because I remember several unexplained deaths at the Schwachter Company."

"Congratulations, Morel," said Alec, bowing. "You have found yourself a believer!"

Stoever spoke seriously, "You idiot—haven't you heard? Charlie was taken by that machine, too. When Morel was in Saint Gallen, the employees of the Schwachter Company started to die. I saw the pictures in magazines. I'll recognize them."

Morel, trembling with anger, left the room. The people had begun to shout at each other.

"There, you see," said Dora. "Now you've hurt his feelings. You must go and find him."

"How could you do a thing like that to Morel!"

"Can't you see? Don't you understand?" insisted Stoever.

"Morel is a nervous man; I don't see why you had to insult him."

"You don't understand!" shouted Stoever angrily. "He took Charlie with his machine, and Charlie died; he took some of the employees at the Schwachter Company, and some of them died mysteriously. Now he says that he has taken us!"

"And we are not dead," said Irene.

"He took himself, too."

"Doesn't anyone understand that it's just a joke?"

"But why is Morel so angry? I've never seen him like this!"

"Well, anyway, Morel has behaved badly," said the man with the protruding teeth. "He should have told us beforehand."

"I'm going to go and find him," said Stoever.

"Stay here!" shouted Dora.

"I'll go," said the man with protruding teeth. "No, I'm not going to make any trouble. I'll just ask him to excuse us and to come back and continue his speech."

They all crowded around Stoever. Excitedly they tried to calm him.

After a while the man with protruding teeth returned. "He won't come," he said. "He asks us to forgive him. I couldn't get him to come back."

Faustine, Dora, and the old woman went out of the room; then some others followed.

Only Alec, the man with protruding teeth, Stoever, and Irene remained. They seemed calm, but very serious. Then they left together.

I heard some people talking in the assembly hall, and others on the stairway. The lights went out and the house was left in the livid light of dawn. I waited, on the alert. There was no noise, there was almost no light. Had they all gone to bed? Or were they lying in wait to capture me? I stayed there, for how long I do not know, trembling, and finally I began to

walk (I believe I did this to hear the sound of my own footsteps and to have evidence of some life), without noticing
that perhaps I was doing exactly what my supposed pursuers
wanted me to do.

I went to the table, put the yellow papers in my pocket. I
saw (and it made me afraid) that the room had no windows,
that I would have to pass through the assembly hall in order
to get out of the building. I walked very slowly; the house
seemed unending. I stood still in the doorway. Finally I
walked slowly, silently, toward an open window; I jumped
out and then I broke into a run.

When I got to the lowlands, I reproached myself for not
having gone away the first day, for wanting to find out about
those mysterious people.

After Morel's explanation, it seemed that this was a plot
organized by the police; I could not forgive myself for being
so slow to understand.

My suspicion may seem absurd, but I believe I can justify
it. Anyone would distrust a person who said, "My companions and I are illusions; we are a new kind of photograph." In
my case the distrust is even more justified: I have been accused of a crime, sentenced to life imprisonment, and it is
possible that my capture is still somebody's profession, his
hope of bureaucratic promotion.

But I was tired, so I went to sleep at once, making vague
plans to escape. This had been a very exciting day.

I dreamed of Faustine. The dream was very sad, very
touching. We were saying good-bye; they were coming to get
her; the ship was about to leave. Then we were alone, saying
a romantic farewell. I cried during the dream and then woke
up feeling miserable and desperate because Faustine was not
there; my only consolation was that we had not concealed
our love. I was afraid that Faustine had gone away while I was
sleeping. I got up and looked around. The ship was gone. My
sadness was profound: it made me decide to kill myself. But

when I glanced up I saw Stoever, Dora, and some of the others on the hillside.

I did not need to see Faustine. I thought then that I was safe: it no longer mattered whether she was there.

I understood that what Morel had said several hours ago was true (but very possibly he did not say it for the first time several hours ago, but several years ago; he repeated it that night because it was part of the week, on the eternal record).

I experienced a feeling of scorn, almost disgust, for these people and their indefatigable, repetitious activity. They appeared many times up there on the edge of the hill. To be on an island inhabited by artificial ghosts was the most unbearable of nightmares; to be in love with one of those images was worse than being in love with a ghost (perhaps we always want the person we love to have the existence of a ghost).

Here are the rest of the yellow papers that Morel did not read:

"I found that my first plan was impossible—to be alone with her and to photograph a scene of my pleasure or of our mutual joy. So I conceived another one, which is, I am sure, better.

"You all know how we discovered this island. Three factors recommended it to me: (1) the tides, (2) the reefs, (3) the light.

"The regularity of the lunar tides and the frequency of the meteorological tides assure an almost constant supply of motive power. The reefs are a vast system to wall out trespassers; the only man who knows them is our captain, McGregor; I have seen to it that he will not have to risk these dangers again. The light is clear but not dazzling—and makes it possible to preserve the images with little or no waste.

"I confess that after I discovered these outstanding virtues, I did not hesitate for an instant to invest my fortune in the purchase of the island and in the construction of the museum, the church, the pool. I rented the cargo ship, which you all call the 'yacht,' so our voyage would be more comfortable.

"The word *museum*, which I use to designate this house, is a survival of the time when I was working on plans for my invention, without knowing how it would eventually turn out. At that time I thought I would build large albums or museums, both public and private, filled with these images.

"Now the time has come to make my announcement: This island, and its buildings, is our private paradise. I have taken some precautions—physical and moral ones—for its defense: I believe they will protect it adequately. Even if we left tomorrow, we would be here eternally, repeating consecutively the moments of this week, powerless to escape from the consciousness we had in each one of them—the thoughts and feelings that the machine captured. We will be able to live a life that is always new, because in each moment of the projection we shall have no memories other than those we had in the corresponding moment of the eternal record, and because the future, left behind many times, will maintain its attributes forever."[6]

They appear from time to time. Yesterday I saw Haynes on the edge of the hill; two days ago I saw Stoever and Irene; today I saw Dora and some of the other women. They make me feel impatient: if I want to live an orderly existence, I must stop looking at these images.

My favorite temptations are to destroy them, to destroy

---

6. *Forever*: as applied to the duration of our immortality: the machine, unadorned and of carefully chosen material, is more incorruptible than the Métro in Paris. (Morel's Note.)

the machines that project them (they must be in the basement), or to break the mill wheel. I control myself; I do not wish to think about my island companions because they could become an obsession.

However, I do not believe there is any danger of that. I am too busy trying to stand the floods, my hunger, the food I eat.

Now I am looking for a way to construct a permanent bed; I shall not find it here in the lowlands; the trees are decayed and cannot support me. But I am determined to change all this: when the tides are high I do not sleep, and the smaller floods interrupt my rest on the other days, but always at a different hour. I cannot get used to these inundations. I find it difficult to sleep, thinking of the moment when the muddy, lukewarm water will cover my face and choke me momentarily. I do not want to be surprised by the current, but fatigue overcomes me and then the water is already there, silently forcing its way into my respiratory passages. This makes me feel painfully tired, and I tend to be irritated and discouraged by the slightest difficulty.

―――

I was reading the yellow papers again. I find that Morel's explanation of the ways to supply certain spatial and temporal needs can lead to confusion. Perhaps it would be better to say: Methods To Achieve Sensory Perceptions, and Methods To Achieve and Retain Such Perceptions. Radio, television, the telephone are exclusively methods of achievement; motion pictures, photography, the phonograph—authentic archives—are methods of achievement and retention.

So then, all the machines that supply certain sensory needs are methods of achievement (before we have the photograph or the phonograph record, it must be taken, recorded).

It is possible that every need is basically spatial, that

somewhere the image, the touch, and the voice of those who are no longer alive must still exist ("nothing is lost—").

This has given me new hope; this is why I am going down to the basement of the museum to look at the machines.

I thought of people who are no longer alive. Someday the men who channel vibrations will assemble them in the world again. I had illusions of doing something like that myself, of inventing a way to put the presences of the dead together again, perhaps. I might be able to use Morel's machine with an attachment that would keep it from receiving the waves from living transmitters (they would no doubt be stronger).

It will be possible for all souls, both those that are intact, and the ones whose elements have been dispersed, to have immortality. But unfortunately the people who have died most recently will be obstructed by the same mass of residue as those who died long ago. To make a single man (who is now disembodied) with all his elements, and without letting an extraneous part enter, one must have the patient desire of Isis when she reconstructed Osiris.

The indefinite conservation of the souls now functioning is assured. Or rather: it will be assured when men understand that they must practice and preach the doctrine of Malthus to defend their place on earth.

It is regrettable that Morel has hidden his invention on this island. I may be mistaken: perhaps Morel is a famous man. If not, I might be able to obtain a pardon from my pursuers as a reward for giving his invention to the world. But if Morel himself did not tell the world about it one of his friends probably did. And yet it is strange that no one spoke of it back in Caracas.

———

I have overcome the nervous repulsion I used to feel toward the images. They do not bother me now. I am living comfortably in the museum, safe from the rising waters. I sleep well, I awake refreshed, and I have recaptured the serenity that made it possible for me to outwit my pursuers and to reach this island.

I must admit that I feel slightly uncomfortable when the images brush against me (especially if I happen to be thinking about something else); but I shall overcome that, too; and the very fact that I can think of other things indicates that my life has become quite normal again.

Now I am able to view Faustine dispassionately, as a simple object. Merely out of curiosity I have been following her for about twenty days. That was not very difficult, although it is impossible to open the doors—even the unlocked ones— (because if they were closed when the scene was recorded, they must be closed when it is projected). I might be able to force them open, but I am afraid that a partial breakage may put the whole machine out of order.

When Faustine goes to her room, she closes the door. There is only one occasion when I am not able to enter without touching her: when Dora and Alec are with her. Then the latter two come out quickly. During the first week I spent that night in the corridor, with my eye at the keyhole of the closed door, but all I could see was part of a blank wall. The next week I wanted to look in from the outside, so I walked along the cornice, exposing myself to great danger, injuring my hands and knees on the rough stone, clinging to it in terror (it is about fifteen feet above the ground). But since the curtains were drawn I was unable to see anything.

The next time I shall overcome my fear and enter the room with Faustine, Dora, and Alec.

The other nights I lie on a mat on the floor, beside her bed. It touches me to have her so close to me, and yet so unaware of this habit of sleeping together that we are acquiring.

A recluse can make machines or invest his visions with reality only imperfectly, by writing about them or depicting them to others who are more fortunate than he.

I think it will be impossible for me to learn anything by looking at the machines: hermetically sealed, they will continue to obey Morel's plan. But tomorrow I shall know for sure. I was not able to go down to the basement today, for I spent the whole afternoon trying to find some food.

If one day the images should fail, it would be wrong to suppose that I have destroyed them. On the contrary, my aim is to save them by writing this diary. Invasions by the sea and invasions by the hordes of increased populations threaten them. It pains me to think that my ignorance, kept intact by the library, which does not have a single book I can use for scientific study, may threaten them too.

I shall not elaborate on the dangers that stalk this island—both the land and the men—because the prophecies of Malthus have been forgotten; and, as for the sea, I must confess that each high tide has caused me to fear that the island may be totally submerged. A fisherman at a bar in Rabaul told me that the Ellice, or Lagoon, Islands are unstable, that some disappear and others emerge from the sea. (Am I in that archipelago? The Sicilian and Ombrellieri are my authorities for believing that I am.)

It is surprising that the invention has deceived the inventor. I too thought that the images were live beings; but my position differed from his: Morel conceived all this; he witnessed and directed the work to its completion, while I saw it in the completed form, already in operation.

The case of the inventor who is duped by his own invention emphasizes our need for circumspection. But I may be generalizing about the peculiarities of one man, moralizing about a characteristic that applies only to Morel.

I approve of the direction he gave, no doubt unconsciously, to his efforts to perpetuate man: but he has preserved nothing

but sensations; and, although his invention was incomplete, he at least foreshadowed the truth: man will one day create human life. His work seems to confirm my old axiom: it is useless to try to keep the whole body alive.

Logical reasons induce us to reject Morel's hopes. The images are not alive. But since his invention has blazed the trail, as it were, another machine should be invented to find out whether the images think and feel (or at least if they have the thoughts and the feelings that the people themselves had when the picture was made; of course, the relationship between their consciousness and these thoughts and feelings cannot be determined). The machine would be very similar to the one Morel invented and would be aimed at the thoughts and sensations of the transmitter; at any distance away from Faustine we should be able to have her thoughts and sensations (visual, auditory, tactile, olfactory, gustatory).

And someday there will be a more complete machine. One's thoughts or feelings during life—or while the machine is recording—will be like an alphabet with which the image will continue to comprehend all experience (as we can form all the words in our language with the letters of the alphabet). Then life will be a repository for death. But even then the image will not be alive; objects that are essentially new will not exist for it. It will know only what it has already thought or felt, or the possible transpositions of those thoughts or feelings.

The fact that we cannot understand anything outside of time and space may perhaps suggest that our life is not appreciably different from the survival to be obtained by this machine.

When minds of greater refinement than Morel's begin to work on the invention, man will select a lonely, pleasant place, will go there with the persons he loves most, and will endure in an intimate paradise. A single garden, if the scenes to be eternalized are recorded at different moments, will contain innumerable paradises, and each group of inhabitants, unaware of the others, will move about simultaneously, almost in the same places, without colliding. But unfortunately these will be vulnerable paradises because the images will not be able to see men; and, if men do not heed the advice of Malthus, someday they will need the land of even the smallest paradise, and will destroy its defenseless inhabitants or will exile them by disconnecting their machines.[7]

I watched them for seventeen days. Not even a man who was in love would have found anything suspect about the conduct of Morel and Faustine.

I do not believe he was referring to her in his speech (although she was the only one who did not laugh at that part). But even though Morel may be in love with Faustine, why should it be assumed that Faustine returns his love?

We can always find a cause for suspicion if we look for it. On one afternoon of the eternal week they walk arm in arm near the palm groves and the museum—but surely there is nothing amiss in that casual stroll.

Because I was determined to live up to my motto, *Ostinato rigore*, I can now say with pride that my vigilance was complete; I considered neither my own comfort nor decorum: I observed what went on under the tables as well as in the open.

---

7. Under the epigraph

   Come, Malthus, and in Ciceronian prose
   Show what a rutting Population grows,
   Until the produce of the Soil is spent,
   And Brats expire for lack of Aliment.

the author writes a lengthy apology, with eloquence and the traditional arguments, for Thomas Robert Malthus and his *Essay on the Principle of Population*. We have omitted it due to lack of space. (Editor's Note.)

One night in the dining room, and another night in the assembly hall, their legs touch. If I attribute that contact to malicious intent, why do I reject the possibility of pure accident?

I repeat: there is no conclusive proof that Faustine feels any love for Morel. Perhaps my own egotism made me suspect that she did. I love Faustine: she is the reason for everything. I am afraid that she loves another man: my mission is to prove that she does not. When I thought that the police were after me, the images on this island seemed to be moving like the pieces in a chess game, following a strategy to capture me.

Morel would be furious, I am sure, if I spread the news of his invention. I do not believe that the fame he might gain would make any difference to him. His friends (including Faustine) would be indignant. But if Faustine had fallen out with Morel—she did not laugh with the others during his speech—then perhaps she would form an alliance with me.

Still it is possible that Morel is dead. If he had died one of his friends would have spread the news of his invention. Or else we should have to postulate a collective death, an epidemic or a shipwreck—which seems quite incredible. But still there is no way to explain the fact that no one knew of the invention when I left Caracas.

One explanation could be that no one believed him, that Morel was out of his mind, or (my original idea) that they were all mad, that the island was a kind of insane asylum.

But those explanations require as much imagination as do the epidemic or the shipwreck.

If I could get to Europe, America, or Asia, I would surely have a difficult time. When I began to be a famous fraud—instead of a famous inventor—Morel's accusations would reach me and then perhaps an order for my arrest would arrive from Caracas. And, worst of all, my perilous situation would have been brought about by the invention of a madman.

But I do not have to run away. It is a stroke of luck to be able to live with the images. If my pursuers should come, they will forget about me when they see these prodigious, inaccessible people. And so I shall stay here.

If I should find Faustine, how she would laugh when I told her about the many times I have talked to her image with tenderness and desperation. But I feel that I should not entertain this thought: and I have written it down merely to set a limit, to see that it holds no charm for me, to abandon it.

A rotating eternity may seem atrocious to an observer, but it is quite acceptable to those who dwell there. Free from bad news and disease, they live forever as if each thing were happening for the first time; they have no memory of anything that happened before. And the interruptions caused by the rhythm of the tides keep the repetition from being implacable.

Now that I have grown accustomed to seeing a life that is repeated, I find my own irreparably haphazard. My plans to alter the situation are useless: I have no next time, each moment is unique, different from every other moment, and many are wasted by my own indolence. Of course, there is no next time for the images either—each moment follows the pattern set when the eternal week was first recorded.

Our life may be thought of as a week of these images—one that may be repeated in adjoining worlds.

Without yielding to my weakness, I can imagine the touching moment when I arrive at Faustine's house, her interest in what I shall tell her, the bond that will be established between us. Perhaps now I am at last on the long and difficult road that leads to Faustine; I know I cannot live without her.

But where does Faustine live? I have been following her for weeks. She speaks of Canada—that is all I know. But

I have another question—and it fills me with horror—is Faustine alive?

Perhaps because the idea of looking for a person whose whereabouts I do not know, a person who may not even be alive, strikes me as being so heartbreaking, so pathetic, Faustine has come to mean more to me than life itself.

How can I go to look for her? The boat is no longer in one piece. The trees are rotten. I am not a good enough carpenter to build a boat out of some other kind of wood, like chairs or doors; in fact, I am not even sure I could have made one from trees. I must wait until I see a ship passing the island. For so long I hoped that one would not come, but now I know I could not return alone. The only ship I have ever seen from this island was Morel's, and that was only the image of a ship.

And if I arrive at my journey's end, if I find Faustine, I shall be in one of the most difficult situations I have ever experienced. Arriving under mysterious circumstances, I shall ask to speak to her alone, and will arouse her suspicions since I shall be a stranger to her. When she discovers that I saw a part of her life, she will think I am trying to gain some dishonest advantage. And when she finds out that I have been sentenced to life imprisonment she will see her worst fears confirmed.

It never occurred to me before that a certain action could bring me good or bad luck. Now, at night, I repeat Faustine's name. Naturally, I like to say it anyway; and even though I am overcome by fatigue I still keep on repeating it (at times I feel nauseated and uneasy, queasy, when I sleep).

When I am less agitated I shall find a way to get away from here. But, in the meantime, writing down what has happened helps me to organize my thoughts. And if I am to die this diary will leave a record of the agony I suffered.

Yesterday there were no images. Desperate in the face of the secret, quiescent machines, I had a presentiment that I would never see Faustine again. But this morning the tide began to rise. I hurried down to the basement, before the images appeared, to try to understand the working of the machines, so I would not be at the mercy of the tides and would be able to make repairs when necessary. I thought that perhaps I might understand the machines if I could see them start, or at least I would get some hint about their structure. But that hope proved to be groundless.

I gained access to the power plant through the opening I had made in the wall, and—(but I must not let myself be carried away by emotion; I must write all this down carefully) I experienced the same surprise and the same exhilaration I felt when I first entered that room. I had the impression of walking through the azure stillness of a river's depths. I sat down to wait, turning my back on the opening I had made (it pained me to see the interruption in the deep-blue continuity of the tile).

How long I stayed there, basking in that beauty, I do not know, but suddenly the green machines lurched into motion. I compared them with the water pump and the motors that produced the light. I looked at them, I listened to them, I fingered them gingerly, but it was no use. My scrutiny was unnecessary, because I knew at once that I was unable to understand the machines. It was as if someone were looking, as if I were trying to cover up my embarrassment or my shame at having hurried to the basement, at having awaited this moment so eagerly.

In my fatigue I have again felt the rush of excitement. Unless I control it, I shall never find a way to leave this place.

This is exactly how it happened: I turned and walked away, with downcast eyes. But when I looked at the wall I was bewildered. I looked for the opening I had made. It was not there.

Thinking that this was just an interesting optical illusion, I stepped to one side to see if it persisted. As if I were blind, I held out my arms and felt all the walls. I bent down to pick up some of the pieces of tile I had knocked off the wall when I made the opening. After touching and retouching that part of the wall repeatedly, I had to accept the fact that it had been repaired.

Could I have been so fascinated by the blue splendor of the room, so interested in the working of the motors, that I did not hear a mason rebuilding the wall?

I moved closer. I felt the coolness of the tile against my ear, and heard an interminable silence, as if the other side had disappeared.

The iron bar that I had used to break the wall was on the floor where I had dropped it the first time I entered the room. "Lucky no one saw it!" I said, pathetically unaware of the situation. "If they had, they probably would have taken it away!"

Again I pressed my ear to this wall that seemed to be intact. Reassured by the silence, I looked for the spot where I had made the opening, and then I began to tap on the wall, thinking that it would be easier to break the fresh plaster. I tapped for a long time, with increasing desperation. The tile was invulnerable. The strongest, most violent blows echoed against the hardness and did not open even a superficial crack or loosen a tiny fragment of the blue glaze.

I rested for a moment and tried to control my nerves.

Then I resumed my efforts, moving to other parts of the wall. Chips fell, and, when large pieces of the wall began to come down, I kept on pounding, bleary-eyed, with an urgency that was far greater than the size of the iron bar, until the resistance of the wall (which seemed unaffected by the force of my repeated pounding) pushed me to the floor, frantic and exhausted. First I saw, then I touched, the pieces of masonry—they were smooth on one side, harsh, earthy on the other;

then, in a vision so lucid it seemed ephemeral and supernatural, my eyes saw the blue continuity of the tile, the undamaged and whole wall, the closed room.

I pounded some more. In some places pieces of the wall broke off, but they did not reveal any sort of cavity. In fact, in the twinkling of an eye the wall was perfect again, achieving that invulnerable hardness I had already observed in the place where I had made the original opening.

I shouted, "Help!" I lunged at the wall several times, and it knocked me down. I had an imbecilic attack of tears. I was overcome by the horror of being in an enchanted place and by the confused realization that its vengeful magic was effective in spite of my disbelief.

Harassed by the terrible blue walls, I looked up at the skylight. I saw, first without understanding and then with fear, a cedar branch split apart and become two branches; then the two branches were fused, as docile as ghosts, to become one branch again. I said out loud or thought very clearly: "I shall never be able to get out. I am in an enchanted place." But then I felt ashamed, like a person who has carried a joke too far, and I understood:

These walls—like Faustine, Morel, the fish in the aquarium, one of the suns and one of the moons, the book by Bélidor—are projections of the machines. They coincide with the walls made by the masons (they are the same walls taken by the machines and then projected on themselves). Where I have broken or removed the first wall, the projected one remains. Since it is a projection nothing can pierce or eliminate it as long as the motors are running.

If I destroy the first wall, the machine room will be open when the motors stop running—it will no longer be a room, but the corner of a room. But when the motors begin again the wall will reappear, and it will be impenetrable.

Morel must have planned the double-wall protection to keep anyone from reaching the machines that control his immortality. But his study of the tides was deficient (it was probably made during a different solar period), and he thought that the power plant would function without any interruptions. Surely he is the one who invented the famous disease that, up to now, has protected the island very well.

My problem is to discover a way to stop the green motors. Perhaps I can find the switch that disconnects them. It took me only one day to learn to operate the light plant and the water pump. I think I shall be able to leave this place.

The skylight is, or will be, my salvation because I shall not resign myself to die of hunger in a state of utter desperation, paying my respects to those I leave behind, as did the Japanese sailor who, with virtuous and bureaucratic agony, faced asphyxiation in a submarine at the bottom of the ocean. The letter he wrote was found in the submarine and printed in the paper. As he awaited death he saluted the Emperor, the ministers, and, in hierarchical order, all the admirals he had time to enumerate. He added comments like: "Now I am bleeding from the nose," or "I feel as if my eardrums have broken."

While writing these details, I had the sensation of living through that experience. I hope I shall not end as he did.

The horrors of the day are written down in my diary. I have filled many pages: now it seems futile to try to find inevitable analogies with dying men who make plans for long futures or who see, at the instant of drowning, a detailed picture of their whole life before them. The final moment must be rapid, confused; we are always so far removed from death that we cannot imagine the shadows that must becloud it. Now I shall stop writing in order to concentrate, serenely, on finding the way to stop these motors. Then the breach will open again, as if by magic, and I shall be outside.

I have not yet been successful in my attempt to stop the motors. My head is aching. Ridiculous attacks of nerves, which I quickly control, rouse me from a progressive drowsiness.

I have the impression, undoubtedly illusory, that if I could receive a little fresh air from the outside I would soon be able to solve these problems. I have tried to break the skylight; like everything else, it is invulnerable.

I keep telling myself that the trouble does not issue from my lethargy or from the lack of air. These motors must be very different from all the others. It seems logical to suppose that Morel designed them so that no one who came to this island would be able to understand them. But the difficulty in running the green motors must stem from their basic difference from the other motors. As I do not understand any of them, this greater difficulty disappears.

Morel's eternity depends on the continued functioning of the motors. I can suppose that they are very solid. Therefore I must control my impulse to break them into pieces. That would only tire me out and use up the air. Writing helps me to control myself.

And what if Morel had thought to photograph the motors—

———

Finally my fear of death freed me from the irrational belief that I was incompetent. I might have seen the motors through a magnifying glass: they ceased to be a meaningless conglomeration of iron and steel; they had forms and arrangements that permitted me to understand their purpose.

I disconnected them. I went outside.

In the machine room, in addition to the water pump and the light plant (which I already mentioned), I recognized:

a) A network of power cables connected to the mill wheel in the lowlands;

b) An assortment of stationary receivers, recorders, and projectors connected to other strategically placed machines that operate throughout the whole island;

c) Three portable machines: receivers, recorders, and projectors for special showings.

Inside of what I had taken for the most important engine (instead it was only a box of tools) I found some incomplete plans that were hard to understand and gave me dubious assistance.

I did not acquire that insight until I had conquered my previous states of mind:

1. Desperation;

2. The feeling that I was playing a dual role, that of actor and spectator. I was obsessed by the idea that I was in a play, awaiting asphyxiation in a submarine at the bottom of the ocean. That state of mind lasted too long; and when I came out of the room night had fallen and it was too dark to look for edible roots.

First I turned on the portable receivers and projectors, the ones for special showings. I focused on flowers, leaves, flies, frogs. I had the thrill of seeing them reproduced in their exact likeness.

Then I committed the imprudence.

I put my left hand in front of the receiver; I turned on the projector and my hand appeared, just my hand, making the lazy movements it made when I photographed it.

Now it is like any other object in the museum.

I am keeping the projector on so that the hand will not disappear. The sight of it is not unpleasant, but rather unusual.

In a story, that hand would be a terrible threat for the protagonist. In reality—what harm can it do?

———

The vegetable transmitters—leaves, flowers—died after five or six hours; the frogs, after fifteen.

The copies survive; they are incorruptible.

I do not know which flies are real and which ones are artificial.

Perhaps the leaves and flowers died because they needed water. I did not give any food to the frogs; and they must have suffered from the unfamiliar surroundings, too.

I suspect that the effects on my hand are the result of my fear of the machine, not of the machine itself. I have a steady, faint burning sensation. Some of my skin has fallen off. Last night I slept fitfully. I imagined horrible changes in my hand. I dreamed that I scratched it, that I broke it into pieces easily. That must have been how I hurt it.

Another day will be intolerable.

First I was curious about a paragraph from Morel's speech. Then I was quite amused, thinking I had made a discovery. I am not sure how that discovery led to this other one, which is judicious, ominous.

I shall not kill myself immediately. When I am most lucid, I tend to postpone my death for one more day, to remain as proof of an amazing combination of ineptitude and enthusiasm (or despair). Perhaps writing down my idea will make it lose its force.

Here is the part of Morel's speech that I found unusual:

"You must forgive me for this rather tedious, unpleasant incident."

Why unpleasant? Because they were going to be told that they had been photographed in a new way, without having been warned beforehand. And naturally the knowledge that a week of one's life, with every detail, had been recorded forever—when that knowledge was imparted after the fact— would be quite a shock!

I also thought: One of these persons must have a dreadful

secret; Morel is either trying to find it out or planning to reveal it.

And then I happened to remember that some people are afraid of having their images reproduced because they believe that their souls will be transferred to the images and they will die.

The thought that Morel had experienced misgivings because he had photographed his friends without their consent amused me; apparently that ancient fear still survived in the mind of my learned contemporary.

I read the sentence again:

"You must forgive me for this rather tedious, unpleasant incident. We shall try to forget it."

What did he mean? That they would soon overlook it, or that they would no longer be able to remember it?

The argument with Stoever was terrible. Stoever's suspicions are the same as mine. I do not know how I could have been so slow to understand.

Another thing: the theory that the images have souls seems to demand, as a basic condition, that the transmitters lose theirs when they are photographed by the machines. As Morel himself says, "The theory that the images have souls seems to be confirmed by the effects of my machine on persons, animals, and vegetables used as transmitters."

A person who would make this statement to his victims must have a very overbearing and audacious conscience, which could be confused with a lack of conscience; but such a monstrosity seems to be in keeping with the man who, following his own idea, organizes a collective death and determines, of his own accord, the common destiny of all his friends.

What was his purpose? To use this rendezvous with his friends to create a kind of private paradise? Or was there some other reason that I have not yet been able to fathom? And if so it very possibly may not interest me.

Now I believe I can identify the dead crew members of the ship that was sunk by the cruiser *Namura*: Morel used his own death and the death of his friends to confirm the rumors about the disease on the island; Morel spread those rumors to protect his machinery, his immortality.

But all this, which I can now view rationally, means that Faustine is dead, that Faustine lives only in this image, for which I do not exist.

———

Then life is intolerable for me. How can I keep on living in the torment of seeming to be with Faustine when she is really so far away? Where can I find her? Away from this island Faustine is lost with the gestures and the dreams of an alien past.

On one of my first pages I said:

"I have the uncomfortable sensation that this paper is changing into a will. If I must resign myself to that, I shall try to make statements that can be verified so that no one, knowing that I was accused of duplicity, will doubt that I was condemned unjustly. I shall adopt the motto of Leonardo —*Ostinato rigore*—as my own,[8] and endeavor to live up to it."

Although I am doomed to misery, I shall not forget that motto.

I shall complete my diary by correcting mistakes and by explaining things I did not understand before. That will be my way of bridging the gap between the ideal of accuracy (which guided me from the start) and my original narration.

The tides: I read the little book by Bélidor (Bernard Forest

———

8. It does not appear at the beginning of the manuscript. Is this omission due to a loss of memory? There is no way to answer that question, and so, as in every doubtful place, we have been faithful to the original. (Editor's Note.)

de). It begins with a general description of the tides. I must confess that the tides on this island seem to follow the explanation given in the book, and not mine. Of course, I never studied tides (only in school, where no one studied), and I described them in the initial chapters of this diary, as they were just beginning to have some importance for me. When I lived on the hill they were no threat. Although I found them interesting, I did not have the time to observe them in detail (there were other dangers to claim my attention then).

According to Bélidor, there are two spring tides each month, at the time of the full moon and the new moon, and two neap tides during the first and third quarters of the moon.

Sometimes a meteorological tide occurred a week after a spring tide (caused by strong winds and rainstorms): surely that was what made me think, mistakenly, that the tides of greater magnitude occur once a week.

Reason for the irregularity of the daily tides: According to Bélidor, the tides rise fifty minutes later each day during the first quarter of the moon, and fifty minutes earlier during the last quarter. But that theory is not completely applicable here: I believe that the rising of the tides must vary from fifteen to twenty minutes each day. Of course, I have no measuring device at my disposal. Perhaps scientists will one day study these tides and make their findings available to the world; then I shall understand them better.

This month there were a number of higher tides; two of them were lunar, and the others, meteorological.

The appearances and disappearances: The machines project the images. The power from the tides causes the machines to operate.

After rather lengthy periods of low tides, there was a series of tides that came up to the mill in the lowlands. The machines began to run, and the eternal record started playing again where it had broken off.

If Morel's speech was on the last night of the week,

the first appearance must have occurred on the night of the third day.

Perhaps the absence of images during the long period before they first appeared was due to the change of the tides with the solar periods.

The two suns and the two moons: Since the week is repeated all through the year, some suns and moons do not coincide (and people complain of the cold when the weather on the island is warm, and swim in fetid water and dance in a thicket or during a storm). And if the whole island were submerged—except for the machines and projectors—the images, the museum, and the island itself would still be visible.

Perhaps the heat of the past few days has been so intense because the temperature of the day when the scene was photographed is superimposed on the present temperature.[9]

Trees and other plant life: The vegetation that was recorded by the machine is withered now; the plants that were not recorded—annuals (flowers, grasses) and the new trees—are luxuriant.

The light switch that did not work, the latches that were impossible to open, the stiff, immovable curtains: What I said before, about the doors, can be applied to the light switch and the latches: When the scene is projected, everything appears exactly as it was during the recording process. And the curtains are stiff for the same reason.

The person who turns out the light: The person who turns out the light in the room across from Faustine's is Morel. He comes in and stands by the bed for a moment. The reader will recall that I dreamed Faustine did this. It irks me to have confused Morel with Faustine.

---

9. The theory of a superimposition of temperatures may not necessarily be false (even a small heater is unbearable on a summer day), but I believe that this is not the real reason. The author was on the island in spring; the eternal week was recorded in summer, and so, while functioning, the machines reflect the temperature of summer. (Editor's Note.)

Charlie. Imperfect ghosts: At first I could not find them. Now I believe I have found their records. But I shall not play them. They could easily shatter my equanimity, and might even prove disastrous for my mental outlook.

The Spaniards I saw in the pantry: They are Morel's servants.

The underground room, the screen of mirrors: I heard Morel say that they are for visual and acoustical experiments.

The French poetry that Stoever recited: I jotted it down:

> Âme, te souvient-il, au fond du paradis,
> De la gare d'Auteuil et des trains de jadis.

Stoever tells the old lady that it is by Verlaine.

And now there is nothing in my diary that has not been explained.[10] Almost everything, in fact, does have an explanation. The remaining chapters will hold no surprises.

I should like to try to account for Morel's behavior.

Faustine tried to avoid him; then he planned the week, the death of all his friends, so that he could achieve immortality with Faustine. That was his compensation for having renounced all of life's possibilities. He realized that death would not be such a disaster for the others, because in exchange for a life of uncertain length, he would give them immortality with their best friends. And Faustine's life too was at his disposal.

But my very indignation is what makes me cautious: Perhaps the hell I ascribe to Morel is really my own. I am the

---

10. He neglected to explain one thing, the most incredible of all: the coexistence, in one space, of an object and its whole image. This fact suggests the possibility that the world is made up exclusively of sensations. (Editor's Note.)

one who is in love with Faustine, who is capable of murder and suicide; I am the monster. Morel may not have been referring to Faustine in his speech; he may have been in love with Irene, Dora, or the old woman.

But I am raving, I am a fool. Of course Morel had no interest in them. He loved the inaccessible Faustine. That is why he killed her, killed himself and all his friends, and invented immortality!

Faustine's beauty deserves that madness, that tribute, that crime. When I denied that, I was too jealous or too stubborn to admit that I loved her.

And now I see Morel's act as something sublime.

My life is not so atrocious. If I abandon my uneasy hopes of going to find Faustine, I can grow accustomed to the idea of spending my life in seraphic contemplation of her.

That way is open to me: to live, to be the happiest of mortals.

But my happiness, like everything human, is insecure. My contemplation of Faustine could be interrupted, although I cannot tolerate the thought of it:

If the machines should break (I do not know how to repair them);

If some doubt should ruin my paradise (certain conversations between Morel and Faustine, some of their glances, could cause persons of less fortitude than I to lose heart);

If I should die.

The real advantage of my situation is that now death becomes the condition and the pawn for my eternal contemplation of Faustine.

I am saved from the interminable minutes necessary to prepare for my death in a world without Faustine; I am saved from an interminable death without Faustine.

When I was ready, I turned on the receivers of simultaneous action. Seven days have been recorded. I performed well: a casual observer would not suspect that I am not a part of the original scene. That came about naturally as the result of my painstaking preparation: I devoted two weeks to continuous study and experiment. I rehearsed my every action tirelessly. I studied what Faustine says, her questions and answers; I often insert an appropriate sentence, so she appears to be answering me. I do not always follow her; I know her movements so well that I usually walk ahead. I hope that, generally, we give the impression of being inseparable, of understanding each other so well that we have no need of speaking.

I am obsessed by the hope of removing Morel's image from the eternal week. I know that it is impossible, and yet as I write these lines I feel the same intense desire, and the same torment. The images' dependence upon each other (especially that of Morel and Faustine) used to annoy me. Now it does not: because I know that, since I have entered that world, Faustine's image cannot be eliminated without mine disappearing too. And—this is the strangest part, the hardest to explain—it makes me happy to know that I depend on Haynes, Dora, Alec, Stoever, Irene, and the others (even on Morel!).

I arranged the records; the machine will project the new week eternally.

An oppressive self-consciousness made me appear unnatural during the first few days of the photographing; now I have overcome that, and, if my image has the same thoughts I had when it was taken, as I believe it does, then I shall spend eternity in the joyous contemplation of Faustine.

I was especially careful to keep my spirit free from worries. I have tried not to question Faustine's actions, to avoid feeling any hatred. I shall have the reward of a peaceful eternity; and I have the feeling that I am really living the week.

The night when Faustine, Dora, and Alec go into the room, I managed to control my curiosity. I did not try to find out what they were doing. Now I am a bit irritated that I left that part unsolved. But in eternity I give it no importance.

I have scarcely felt the progression of my death; it began in the tissues of my left hand; it has advanced greatly and yet it is so gradual, so continuous, that I do not notice it.

I am losing my sight. My sense of touch has gone; my skin is falling off; my sensations are ambiguous, painful; I try not to think about them.

When I stood in front of the screen of mirrors, I discovered that I have no beard, I am bald. I have no nails on my fingers or toes, and my flesh is tinged with rose. My strength is diminishing. I have an absurd impression of the pain: it seems to be increasing, but I feel it less.

My persistent, deplorable preoccupation with Morel's relationship to Faustine keeps me from paying much attention to my own destruction; that is an unexpected and beneficent result.

Unfortunately, not all my thoughts are so useful: in my imagination I am plagued by the hope that my illness is pure autosuggestion; that the machines are harmless; that Faustine is alive and that soon I shall find her; that together we shall laugh at these false signs of impending death; that I shall take her to Venezuela, to another Venezuela. For my own country, with its leaders, its troops with rented uniforms and deadly aim, threatens me with constant persecution on the roads, in the tunnels, in the factories. But I still love you, my Venezuela, and I have saluted you many times since the start of my disintegration: for you are also the days when I worked on the literary magazine—a group of men (and I, a

wide-eyed, respectful boy) inspired by the poetry of Orduño—
an ardent literary school that met in restaurants or on bat-
tered trolleys. My Venezuela, you are a piece of cassava bread
as large as a shield and uninfested by insects. You are the
flooded plains, with bulls, mares, and jaguars being carried
along by the swift current. And you, Elisa, I see you standing
there, you and the Chinese laundrymen who helped me, and
in each memory you seem more like Faustine: you told them
to take me to Colombia and we crossed the high plateau in
the bitter cold; the Chinamen covered me with thick velvety
leaves so I would not freeze to death; while I look at Faustine,
I shall not forget you—and I thought I did not love you! I remember that when the imperious Valentín Gómez read us
the declaration of independence on July 5 in the elliptical
room of the Capitol we (Orduño and the others) showed our
defiance by turning to stare at Tito Salas's painting of General
Bolívar crossing the Colombian border. But when the band
played our national anthem, we could not suppress our patri-
otic emotion, the emotion I cannot suppress now.

But my rigid discipline must never cease to combat those
ideas, for they jeopardize my ultimate calm.

I can still see my image moving about with Faustine. I
have almost forgotten that it was added later; anyone would
surely believe we were in love and completely dependent
on each other. Perhaps the weakness of my eyes makes the
scenes appear this way. In any case, it is consoling to die
while watching such satisfactory results.

My soul has not yet passed to the image; if it had, I would
have died, I (perhaps) would no longer see Faustine, and
would be with her in a vision that no one can ever destroy.

To the person who reads this diary and then invents a
machine that can assemble disjoined presences, I make this
request: Find Faustine and me, let me enter the heaven of her
consciousness. It will be an act of piety.

OTHER NEW YORK REVIEW BOOKS CLASSICS*

For a complete list of titles, visit www.nyrb.com.

DAVID JONES In Parenthesis
ERNST JÜNGER The Glass Bees
TÉTÉ-MICHEL KPOMASSIE An African in Greenland
D. B. WYNDHAM LEWIS AND CHARLES LEE (EDITORS)
The Stuffed Owl: An Anthology of Bad Verse
GEORG CHRISTOPH LICHTENBERG The Waste Books
H. P. LOVECRAFT AND OTHERS The Colour Out of Space
JANET MALCOLM In the Freud Archives
JAMES MCCOURT Mawrdew Czgowchwz
HENRI MICHAUX Miserable Miracle
NANCY MITFORD Madame de Pompadour
ALBERTO MORAVIA Boredom
ALBERTO MORAVIA Contempt
ÁLVARO MUTIS The Adventures and Misadventures of Maqroll
L. H. MYERS The Root and the Flower
DARCY O'BRIEN A Way of Life, Like Any Other
IONA AND PETER OPIE The Lore and Language of Schoolchildren
BORIS PASTERNAK, MARINA TSVETAYEVA, AND RAINER MARIA RILKE
Letters: Summer 1926
CESARE PAVESE The Moon and the Bonfires
CESARE PAVESE The Selected Works of Cesare Pavese
ANDREI PLATONOV The Fierce and Beautiful World
J. F. POWERS Morte d'Urban
J. F. POWERS The Stories of J. F. Powers
J. F. POWERS Wheat That Springeth Green
RAYMOND QUENEAU We Always Treat Women Too Well
RAYMOND QUENEAU Witch Grass
JEAN RENOIR Renoir, My Father
FR. ROLFE Hadrian the Seventh
WILLIAM ROUGHEAD Classic Crimes
DANIEL PAUL SCHREBER Memoirs of My Nervous Illness
JAMES SCHUYLER Alfred and Guinevere
LEONARDO SCIASCIA To Each His Own
LEONARDO SCIASCIA The Wine-Dark Sea
SHCHEDRIN The Golovlyov Family
GEORGES SIMENON Dirty Snow
GEORGES SIMENON Three Bedrooms in Manhattan
MAY SINCLAIR Mary Olivier: A Life
TESS SLESINGER The Unpossessed: A Novel of the Thirties
CHRISTINA STEAD Letty Fox: Her Luck
STENDHAL The Life of Henry Brulard
ITALO SVEVO As a Man Grows Older
A. J. A. SYMONS The Quest for Corvo
EDWARD JOHN TRELAWNY Records of Shelley, Byron, and the Author
LIONEL TRILLING The Middle of the Journey
IVAN TURGENEV Virgin Soil
ROBERT WALSER Jakob von Gunten
ROBERT WALSER Selected Stories
SYLVIA TOWNSEND WARNER Lolly Willowes
SYLVIA TOWNSEND WARNER Mr. Fortune's Maggot *and* The Salutation
GLENWAY WESCOTT The Pilgrim Hawk
REBECCA WEST The Fountain Overflows
PATRICK WHITE Riders in the Chariot
EDMUND WILSON To the Finland Station